T0345623

NEW LONGMAN LITERATURE

Different Cultures

A Collection of Short Stories

Stories selected and arranged by Roy Blatchford
Notes: Steve Willshaw

PEARSON
Longman
Edinburgh Gate
Harlow, Essex

Pearson Education Limited
Edinburgh Gate
Harlow
Essex
CM20 2JE
England

This educational edition first published by Pearson Education 2003

31

ISBN 978-0-582-48850-2

Printed in Great Britain by Bell and Bain Ltd, Glasgow

The Publisher's policy is to use paper manufactured from sustainable
forests.

Editorial notes by Steve Willshaw

Cover photograph © Don Hammond/CORBIS

Contents

My Simple Little Brother and the Great Aversion Therapy Experiment

Lilith Norman

There is no one in the whole wide world quite as stupid as my young brother, Fields. Fieldsy is seven now, and our sister, Lee, is sixteen. I'm almost in the middle, and my name is Paddy, short for Paddock. Our surname is Meadows, you see, and Dad gave us these names because he thinks he is some sort of funny man. Ha! ha!

But to get back to young Fieldsy. There is only one word for him: d-u-m-b. DUMB!

We first discovered this as soon as Fieldsy was old enough to talk – or to understand what other people were saying, which was even earlier. All little kids do some pretty weird things, and we used to think Fieldsy was just doing the normal strange experiments kids do do as they try to find out what the world is all about and how things work. It was only when Fieldsy could talk properly and let us know what passed for thought processes in that skull of his that we realized Fieldsy was blessed with a rich weirdness all his own.

For instance, Fieldsy was terrified of rain. I mean terrified! At the first drop he'd come hurtling inside at something faster than the speed of light and go to ground under his bed. Mum tried to drag him out and comfort him the first couple of dozen times, but Fieldsy just hooked his fingers through the bedsprings and clung on, screaming, 'No! No! No!'

'Leave him be,' said Dad crossly, as he watched Mum crawling about in the dust under the bed for what must have been the twenty-fifth time. 'Don't coddle the child. He'll grow out of it.'

It was only when Fieldsy was able to talk properly that we found out what the trouble was. It wasn't the noise of the rain on the galvanized roof, as Lee had thought. (I could have told her that, and I did! Fieldsy reacted just the same even if the nearest galvanized roof was seventeen miles away.) No, it was something Dad had said when Fieldsy was only a toddler.

I can remember the long, dry summer we had had that year, but at last the clouds had banked up heavily in the southwest. You knew there was a corker of a storm coming – rain, hail, wind, the lot. Dad had got up from afternoon tea, cocked an eye at the weather, and said, in all innocence: 'I think I'll lock the hens into the shed early. It's going to rain buckets any minute now.'

That was Fieldsy's problem. As soon as the first drop hit him he had to hide away from the great deluge of buckets likely to clank down on his unprotected head. The fact that no buckets had yet fallen only made their likelihood even likelier in the next storm. Logic was never Fieldsy's strong point.

Do you need another example? There was the time Dad came home from the markets with a bulging wallet because he'd just sold a mob of heifers. The next thing he knew, the wallet was missing. So was Fieldsy. Dad found them together, naturally. Fieldsy was carefully pulling the

2

notes out of the wallet one by one, and stuffing them down the grease-trap outside the kitchen sink. Why? When Dad's face had changed back from stormy purple to pale mauve that's what he wanted to know too.

It was so simple that only Fieldsy could have thought of it. Mum and Dad had been discussing what they would spend the money on. Mum had wanted a new washing-machine. Dad thought he might get the old sulky done up so that he could enter in the harness-horse section of the local show. Dad fancied himself a bit that way too, just as he fancied himself a comedian. In the end Mum had given in, with a very bad grace, and had said (her exact words): 'Well, if you want to throw your money down the drain, don't let me stop you!'

So Fieldsy was only trying to help. Of course, Dad had to take the grease-trap apart, and Mum had to launder the notes. For a little while we were probably the only house in Australia with several hundred dollars pegged to our clothes line.

After that episode we all got stuck into Fieldsy. We tried to explain that a lot of the things that people say are only words: phrases that don't really mean what they seem to mean. Fieldsy listened to each of us in turn. Dad, Mum, Lee, and me. He frowned, he nodded his head, and once or twice he said crossly, *'I know that!'*

Heaven knows what was really going on in that bit of solid bone behind Fieldsy's face, for despite his agreement we didn't make any progress at all. In fact it got worse, for Fieldsy now entered what we called his 'gruesome' phase.

3

It started a few weeks ago. We were having steak and kidney pudding for dinner. It looked luscious, with the steam rising from the white puddingy part – and the sort of smell that made you almost swoon at the thought of eating it. Mum served it up and started passing the plates round the table. Dad set his down, picked up his knife and fork, and inhaled with the sort of snort a horse makes when you drag it away from the trough.

'That is the best-looking steak and kidney pudding I've ever seen,' said Dad.

'It should be,' said Mum, smirking at Lee. 'It's a very special pudding, because Lee had a hand in making it.'

Well, that was enough for young Fieldsy. He turned white, then green. I was just passing him his plate, so I saw it all. Fieldsy just shook his head, clenched his teeth, and clamped his mouth shut tighter than a zipper. It didn't matter that Lee showed Fieldsy she still had two apparently normal hands. Maybe he thought she'd bought a plastic one and stuck it on, but he wouldn't touch the steak and kidney. Not that I worried, because I gobbled up his helping as well as my own. After all, if someone's dumb enough to turn down Mum's cooking …!

But it was the second bit of grue that led to the showdown. It might have been funny afterwards, but it certainly wasn't at the time. It started when Dad went to the sales to buy some bullocks, and this stray dog came running up, barking like a fool, just as Dad was driving the bullocks into the trailer. Bullocks went every which way, and in the flurry Dad got wedged against the side of the rails and broke his leg.

Mum was telling us all about it over dinner that night. 'It would never have happened if your father hadn't lost his head,' she said.

That did it. Fieldsy was off, weeping and carrying on a treat. Mum tried to explain that it was just a saying. Dad wasn't really lying in the hospital, one leg in plaster and no head to put on his pillow. It was no use. She just couldn't get through to Dumbbell. None of us could. Next day Fieldsy refused to go with us to visit Dad. Not that I blame him. I wouldn't like the idea of seeing a headless father lying about either.

But it was Dad's accident that led to 'the great aversion therapy experiment'. With Dad out of action, we needed someone to help run the farm, so Mum phoned Dad's brother, Uncle Percy. Uncle Percy was older than Dad, and the farm should have been his, but he had signed it all over to Dad and gone to the city to study. He said the only way to make anything of yourself these days was to get qualifications. Once you were qualified, the world was your oyster.

The trouble was, Uncle Percy was still getting qualified after thirty years. He even looked the part. Flared jeans, a T-shirt with POLITICIANS ARE MADE OF PLASTIC on the front of it, and stringy shoulder-length hair. (He's lucky there, because Dad is already as bald as Ayers Rock even though he's ten years younger than Uncle Percy.) The one thing wrong with Uncle Percy's gear was Uncle Percy – he's only about five foot six, and round as a keg – so he looked a bit odd.

But he certainly has qualifications. He has enough certificates and degrees and diplomas to sink a fair-sized fleet, but there is always one more he had to get 'just to make sure'. He's a fully-qualified vet, and a Doctor of Philosophy; a fitter and turner, an archaeologist, and an expert on conchology. He's got diplomas in agriculture and town planning, and a commercial pilot's licence; he's studied wine-making and Ancient Egyptian and psychology, and dozens of other things. It was that last bit that was to prove our downfall, though. Psychology,

As soon as Uncle Percy arrived he insisted we all go to see Dad for 'a family conference'. So Mum had to explain about young Fieldsy and his distorted view of the world. It took her three hours by the time she remembered all Fieldsy's idiocies!

'Stuff and nonsense,' snorted Uncle Percy. 'You're handling the boy all wrong. What you should use is aversion therapy.'

We all looked blank except Fieldsy – he was playing outside.

So Uncle Percy explained what aversion therapy was. 'It's the treatment they use on alcoholics,' he said. I could see Mum beginning to clench her teeth, a sure sign she was getting mad. I guess it is upsetting to have your darling youngest son discussed as though he is really sick, even when he is a bit strange in the head. Uncle Percy

6

ploughed on regardless. 'What they do is give the subject an electric shock every time he starts to take a drink.'

'You are *not* going to give *my* son electric shocks!' snapped Mum.

Uncle Percy saw the glint in her eye and backtracked hastily. 'No, no. Nothing as drastic as that. But don't you see, it's just because the things Fields expects to happen never *do* happen that he persists in his – er – delusion? Now, if he could once have one of these silly phrases come true I think the shock would snap him out of it for good. It's what he *imagines* that is so much worse than what he would actually see.'

Well, we argued back and forth for another hour or so, and at last Mum agreed. But only on condition that there would be absolutely no electric shocks, and no physical damage of any sort. She didn't seem to worry so much about mental damage, but I did. After all, there's not much between Fieldsy's ears, and what there is seems pretty precariously balanced to me. Anyway, it was finally agreed that the great aversion therapy experiment would take place the next day, as soon as Uncle Percy had bought the necessary equipment. I agreed to be the muggins who would start it all off.

The next day was a Saturday, and straight after lunch I went into action. I took Fieldsy aside and put on my solemnest face. 'Now, you've got to be especially good while Uncle Percy is here,' I said. 'No mucking up. Because whatever you do, Uncle Percy will know. *He's got eyes in the back of his head!'*

7

Fieldsy stared at me, his jaw slowly sinking down like a faulty pump-handle. 'Gee!' he whispered at last, as the wonder of Uncle Percy's physical endowment gradually sank in.

'Sure,' I said. 'Didn't you know that?' Fieldsy shook his head dumbly. 'Well, if you don't believe me, sneak out and have a look. He's out on the verandah having a doze.'

Fieldsy stared at me for a long minute. Then he turned and tiptoed to the verandah where Uncle Percy had planted himself as planned. Fieldsy sneaked up behind him. Uncle Percy had let his head fall forward on to his chest so that Fieldsy could have a good look at the back of his head. Fieldsy's hand inched out, paused, inched on, until he was just touching Uncle Percy's long black locks. He turned then to look at me and I nodded encouragingly. Fieldsy turned back and began to part Uncle Percy's hair.

Suddenly he froze. His hands clenched and he gave a sort of ultrasonic yip. There were two great china eyes staring at him. Then everything happened at once. Fieldsy, his hands still clenched in terror, turned to run. There was a tattering tear, like the sound of a sheet of sticking plaster being ripped off a table top, and the whole of Uncle Percy's hair came away. As it jerked free the strands of hair bounced apart again, showing those two staring, china-white eyes. Fieldsy thought they were coming after him. He gave another strangled yip and flung his hands over *his* eyes to blot out the horrible sight. The inside of the wig, still well-covered with adhesive, transferred itself to

Fieldsy's forehead and stuck there back to front, with Uncle Percy's locks covering Fieldsy's face like a veil.

All this time Uncle Percy was screeching like a jet taking off in a bottle. And me? I just stood there, solidified. At first I thought Uncle Percy had been well and truly scalped. It was only when the hair stuck fast to Fieldsy that the penny dropped and I realized the old phony had been wearing a wig all along.

Meanwhile Fieldsy, finding himself enveloped in fronds of hairy darkness, turned and floundered his way to the back door. Once outside he took off across the paddock towards town. Perhaps he thought that if he could run far enough and fast enough he could get away from whatever was trying to swallow him. By the time I had unfrozen and reached the back door myself, Fieldsy was half-way across the paddock. .

Near the fowl yard he fell over the chopping block, and he covered about twenty yards on his hands and knees before his own momentum brought him back to his feet. Unfortunately the hens saw him – a four-legged *something* with a mask of black hair scuttling towards them. The hens, being even less well-balanced mentally than Fieldsy, panicked.

'Fo-o-x! Fox-fox-fox!' they shrieked, and headed for the highest branches they could find, lurching upwards with straining wings and a shower of falling feathers. (The shock turned them all off the lay for a month.)

Fieldsy kept on going.

His way lay right in line with the weedy little creek that formed our boundary, but nothing could stop him now. He plunged into the creek, went under briefly, came up spluttering, and splashed across. The wig was now plastered flat to his face, in strands, like the slats of a picket fence, and the china eyeballs clonked on his cheekbones. Chickweed and mud hung all about him.

Then he hit the highway into town, and the feel of the firm asphalt let him put on an extra burst of speed. It was only half a mile into town and Fieldsy covered it in record time. The main street was deserted. All the adults were at home, all the kids were at the pictures. The only shop open was the milk bar beside the pictures.

As Fieldsy reached the milk bar he was slowing down. He was puffing hard, and he had to limit himself to a fast walk. Mick, the owner of the milk bar, was lounging at the entrance, waiting for the rush of kids at interval, when he saw Fieldsy coming, and came out to help him.

'Whatsamatter, kid?' he asked, grabbing Fieldsy by the arm. Fieldsy, certain the monster had caught him at last, tore himself free and fled into the nearest doorway to hide. It happened to be the cinema.

He blundered on, through one door and then another. He tore down the aisle, found his way up the stairs to the stage, and teetered along in front of the screen. He was puffing and blowing even more now, and giving little grunting calls for help. For a few minutes he was silhouetted against the screen: a faceless, gibbering *thing*, with great staring white eyeballs gleaming in the light from the projector, a second pair of smaller beady eyeballs (his own) just above them and with horrible dripping tentacles.

It was unfortunate that the film he interrupted was *Slime Man from Saturn*, for the audience gave one unanimous scream of terror, rose to their feet with a crashing up of seats, and fled in all directions.

It took quite a while to collect them all and herd them back into the theatre. Even when they saw what the monster really was, some of them refused to go back. A few of the more timid ones have never gone to the pictures again.

I reached the theatre just as kids and adults shot out every which way. There was no sign of Fieldsy, but I felt somehow that the uproar must have something to do with him. I fought my way in against the tide, and found Fieldsy sitting in the front row of the stalls enjoying the film. The water from the creek had finally softened the glue on the wig and it had fallen off. Fieldsy, free at last, and rather startled to find himself at the pictures, had decided to take advantage of his good fortune, for Mum never lets him go to horror films.

When Fieldsy and I got home (with the wig, which I found lying on the stage) Uncle Percy took it without a word. Mum offered to put it through the washing-machine, but Uncle Percy just took it away and hid it at the bottom of his suitcase. He goes around in his scalp now, and he looks better for it. He's even talking seriously of getting a job and putting some of his many qualifications to work. After his aversion therapy experiment he's beginning to feel that all theory and no practice may not be enough.

And Fieldsy? Did the great aversion therapy experiment work? Well, I'll let you figure that out for yourself. But if you want to know what the gruesome little monster is doing right this minute, I'll tell you. He's down in the paddock with my fat old pony, Skimble, watching him like a hawk. Why? Because Dad said at breakfast this morning that all Skimble does these days is stand around eating his head off.

Rules of the Game

Amy Tan

I was six when my mother taught me the art of invisible strength. It was a strategy for winning arguments, respect from others, and eventually, though neither of us knew it at the time, chess games.

'Bite back your tongue,' scolded my mother when I cried loudly, yanking her hand toward the store that sold bags of salted plums. At home, she said, 'Wise guy, he not go against the wind. In Chinese we say, Come from South, blow with wind – poom! – North will follow. Strongest wind cannot be seen.'

The next week I bit back my tongue as we entered the store with the forbidden candies. When my mother finished her shopping, she quietly plucked a small bag of plums from the rack and put it on the counter with the rest of the items.

My mother imparted her daily truths so she could help my older brothers and me rise above our circumstances. We lived in San Francisco's Chinatown. Like most of the other Chinese children who played in the back alleys of restaurants and curio shops, I didn't think we were poor. My bowl was always full, three five-course meals every day, beginning with a soup full of mysterious things I didn't want to know the names of.

We lived on Waverly Place, in a warm, clean, two-bedroom flat that sat above a small Chinese bakery specializing in steamed pastries and dim sum. In the early morning, when the alley was still quiet, I could smell fragrant red beans as they were cooked down to a pasty sweetness. By daybreak, our flat was heavy with the odor of fried sesame balls and sweet curried chicken crescents. From my bed, I would listen as my father got ready for work, then locked the door behind him, one-two-three clicks.

At the end of our two-block alley was a small sandlot playground with swings and slides well-shined down the middle with use. The play area was bordered by wood-slat benches where old-country people sat cracking roasted watermelon seeds with their golden teeth and scattering the husks to an impatient gathering of gurgling pigeons. The best playground, however, was the dark alley itself. It was crammed with daily mysteries and adventures. My brothers and I would peer into the medicinal herb shop, watching old Li dole out onto a stiff sheet of white paper the right amount of insect shells, saffron-colored seeds and pungent leaves for his ailing customers. It was said that he once cured a woman dying of an ancestral curse that had eluded the best of American doctors. Next to the pharmacy was a printer who specialized in gold-embossed wedding invitations and festive red banners.

Farther down the street was Ping Yuen Fish Market. The front window displayed a tank crowded with doomed fish and turtles struggling to gain footing on the slimy green-tiled sides. A hand-written sign informed tourists, 'Within this store, is all for food, not for pet.' Inside, the butchers with their bloodstained white smocks deftly gutted the fish while customers cried out their orders and shouted, 'Give me your freshest,' to which the butchers always protested, 'All are freshest.' On less crowded market days, we would inspect the crates of live frogs and crabs which we were warned not to poke, boxes of dried cuttlefish, and row upon row of iced prawns, squid and slippery fish. The sanddabs made me shiver each time; their eyes lay on one flattened side and reminded me of my mother's story of a careless girl who ran into a crowded street and was crushed by a cab. 'Was smash flat,' reported my mother.

At the corner of the alley was Hong Sing's, a four-table café with a recessed stairwell in front that led to a door marked 'Tradesmen'. My brothers and I believed the bad people emerged from this door at night. Tourists never went to Hong Sing's, since the menu was printed only in Chinese. A Caucasian man with a big camera once posed me and my playmates in front of the restaurant. He had us move to the side of the picture window so the photo would capture the roasted duck with its head dangling from a juice-covered rope. After he took the picture, I told him he should go into Hong Sing's and eat dinner. When he smiled and asked me what they served, I shouted, 'Guts and duck's feet and octopus gizzards!' Then I ran off with my friends, shrieking with laughter as we scampered across the alley and hid in the entryway grotto of the

China Gem Company, my heart pounding with hope that he would chase us.

My mother named me after the street that we lived on: Waverly Place Jong, my official name for important American documents. But my family called me Meimei, 'Little Sister'. I was the youngest, the only daughter. Each morning before school, my mother would twist and yank on my thick black hair until she had formed two tightly wound pigtails. One day, as she struggled to weave a hard-toothed comb through my disobedient hair, I had a sly thought.

I asked her, 'Ma, what is Chinese torture?' My mother shook her head. A bobby pin was wedged between her lips. She wetted her palm and smoothed the hair above my ear, then pushed the pin in so that it nicked sharply against my scalp.

'Who say this word?' she asked without a trace of knowing how wicked I was being. I shrugged my shoulders and said, 'Some boy in my class said Chinese people do Chinese torture.'

'Chinese people do many things,' she said simply. 'Chinese people do business, do medicine, do painting. Not lazy like American people. We do torture. Best torture.'

My older brother Vincent was the one who actually got the chess set. We had gone to the annual Christmas party held at the First Chinese Baptist Church at the end of the alley. The missionary ladies had put together a Santa bag of gifts donated by members of another church. None of the gifts had names on them. There were separate sacks for boys and girls of different ages.

One of the Chinese parishioners had donated a Santa Claus costume and a stiff paper beard with cotton balls glued to it. I think the only children who thought he was the real thing were too young to know that Santa Claus was not Chinese. When my turn came up, the Santa man asked me how old I was. I thought it was a trick question; I was seven according to the American formula and eight by the Chinese calendar. I said I was born on March 17, 1951. That seemed to satisfy him. He then solemnly asked if I had been a very, very good girl this year and did I believe in Jesus Christ and obey my parents. I knew the only answer to that. I nodded back with equal solemnity.

Having watched the other children opening their gifts, I already knew that the big gifts were not necessarily the nicest ones. One girl my age got a large coloring book of biblical characters, while a less greedy girl who selected a smaller box received a glass vial of lavender toilet water. The sound of the box was also important. A ten-year-old boy had chosen a box that jangled when he shook it. It was a tin globe of the world with a slit for inserting money. He must have thought it was full of dimes and nickels, because when he saw that it had just ten pennies, his face fell with such undisguised disappointment that his mother slapped the side of his head and led him out of the church hall, apologizing to the crowd for her son who had such bad manners he couldn't appreciate such a fine gift.

As I peered into the sack, I quickly fingered the remaining presents, testing their weight, imagining what they contained. I chose a heavy, compact one that was wrapped in shiny silver foil and a red satin ribbon. It was a twelve-pack of Life Savers and I spent the rest of the party arranging and rearranging the candy tubes in the order of my favorites. My brother Winston chose wisely as well. His present turned out to be a box of intricate plastic parts; the instructions on the box proclaimed that when they were properly assembled he would have an authentic miniature replica of a World War II submarine.

Vincent got the chess set, which would have been a very decent present to get at a church Christmas party, except it was obviously used and, as we discovered later, it was missing a black pawn and a white knight. My mother graciously thanked the unknown benefactor, saying, 'Too good. Cost too much.' At which point, an old lady with fine white, wispy hair nodded toward our family and said with a whistling whisper, 'Merry, merry Christmas.'

When we got home, my mother told Vincent to throw the chess set away. 'She not want it. We not want it,' she said, tossing her head stiffly to the side with a tight, proud smile. My brothers had deaf ears. They were already lining up the chess pieces and reading from the dog-eared instruction book.

I watched Vincent and Winston play during Christmas week. The chessboard seemed to hold elaborate secrets waiting to be untangled. The chessmen were more powerful than old Li's magic herbs that cured ancestral curses. And my brothers wore such serious faces that I was sure something was at stake that was greater than avoiding the tradesmen's door to Hong Sing's.

'Let me! Let me!' I begged between games when one brother or the other would sit back with a deep sigh of relief and victory, the other annoyed, unable to let go of the outcome. Vincent at first refused to let me play, but when I offered my Life Savers as replacements for the buttons that filled in for the missing pieces, he relented. He chose the flavors: wild cherry for the black pawn and peppermint for the white knight. Winner could eat both.

As our mother sprinkled flour and rolled out small doughy circles for the steamed dumplings that would be our dinner that night, Vincent explained the rules, pointing to each piece: 'You have sixteen pieces and so do I. One king and queen, two bishops, two knights, two castles and eight pawns. The pawns can only move forward one step, except on the first move. Then they can move two. But they can only take men by moving crossways like this, except in the beginning, when you can move ahead and take another pawn.

'Why?' I asked as I moved my pawn. 'Why can't they move more steps?'

'Because they're pawns,' he said.

'But why do they go crossways to take other men? Why aren't there any women and children?'

'Why is the sky blue? Why must you always ask stupid questions?' asked Vincent. 'This is a game. These are the rules. I didn't make them up. See. Here. In the book.' He jabbed a page with a pawn in his hand. 'Pawn. P-A-W-N. Pawn. Read it yourself.'

My mother patted the flour off her hands. 'Let me see book,' she said quietly. She scanned the pages quickly, not reading the foreign symbols, seeming to search deliberately for nothing in particular.

'This American rules,' she concluded at last. 'Every time people come out from foreign country, must know rules. You not know, judge say, Too bad, go back. They not telling you why so you can use their way go forward. They say, Don't know why, you find out yourself. But they knowing all the time. Better you take it, find out why yourself.' She tossed her head back with a satisfied smile.

I found out about all the whys later. I read the rules and looked up all the big words in a dictionary. I borrowed books from the China-town library. I studied each chess piece, trying to absorb the power each contained.

I learned about opening moves and why it's important to control the centre early on; the shortest distance between two points is straight down the middle. I learned about the middle game and why tactics between two adversaries are like clashing ideas; the one who plays better has the clearest plans for both attacking and getting out of traps. I learned why it is essential in the endgame to have foresight, a mathematical understanding of all possible moves, and patience; all weaknesses and advantages become evident to a strong adversary and are obscured to a tiring opponent. I discovered that for the whole game one must gather invisible strengths and see the endgame before the game begins.

I also found out why I should never reveal 'why' to others. A little knowledge withheld is a great advantage one should store for future use. That is the power of chess. It is a game of secrets in which one must show and never tell.

I loved the secrets I found within the sixty-four black and white squares. I carefully drew a handmade chessboard and pinned it to the wall next to my bed, where at night I would stare for hours at imaginary battles. Soon I no longer lost any games or Life Savers, but I lost my adversaries. Winston and Vincent decided they were more interested in roaming the streets after school in their Hopalong Cassidy cowboy hats.

On a cold spring afternoon, while walking home from school, I detoured through the playground at the end of our alley. I saw a group of old men, two seated across a folding table playing a game of chess, others smoking pipes, eating peanuts and watching. I ran home and grabbed Vincent's chess set, which was bound in a cardboard box with rubber bands. I also carefully selected two prized rolls of Life Savers. I came back to the park and approached a man who was observing the game.

'Want to play?' I asked him. His face widened with surprise and he grinned as he looked at the box under my arm.

'Little sister, been a long time since I play with dolls,' he said, smiling benevolently. I quickly put the box down next to him on the bench and displayed my retort.

Lau Po, as he allowed me to call him, turned out to be a much better player than my brothers. I lost many games and many Life Savers. But over the weeks, with each diminishing roll of candies, I added new secrets. Lau Po gave me the names. The Double Attack from the East and West Shores. Throwing Stones on the Drowning Man. The Sudden Meeting of the Clan. The Surprise from the Sleeping Guard. The Humble Servant Who Kills the King. Sand in the Eyes of Advancing Forces. A Double Killing Without Blood.

There were also the fine points of chess etiquette. Keep captured men in neat rows, as well-tended prisoners. Never announce 'Check' with vanity, lest someone with an unseen sword slit your throat. Never hurl pieces into the sandbox after you have lost a game, because then you must find them again, by yourself, after apologizing to all around you. By the end of the summer, Lau Po had taught me all he knew, and I had become a better chess player.

A small weekend crowd of Chinese people and tourists would gather as I played and defeated my opponents one by one. My mother would join the crowds during these outdoor exhibition games. She sat proudly on the bench, telling my admirers with proper Chinese humility, 'Is luck.'

A man who watched me play in the park suggested that my mother allow me to play in local chess tournaments. My mother smiled graciously, an answer that meant nothing. I desperately wanted to go, but bit back my tongue. I knew she would not let me play among strangers. So as we walked home I said in a small voice that I didn't want to play in the local tournament. They would have American rules. If I lost, I would bring shame on my family.

'Is shame you fall down nobody push you,' said my mother.

During my first tournament, my mother sat with me in the front row as I waited for my turn. I frequently bounced my legs to unstick them from the cold metal seat of the folding chair. When my name was called, I leapt up. My mother unwrapped something in her lap. It was her *chang*, a small tablet of red jade which held the sun's fire. 'Is luck,' she whispered and tucked it into my dress pocket. I turned to my opponent, a fifteen-year-old boy from Oakland. He looked at me, wrinkling his nose.

As I began to play, the boy disappeared, the color ran out of the room and I saw only my white pieces and his black ones waiting on the other side. A light wind began blowing past my ears. It whispered secrets only I could hear.

'Blow from the South,' it murmured. 'The wind leaves no trail.' I saw a clear path, the traps to avoid. The crowd rustled. 'Shhh! Shhh!' said the corners of the room. The wind blew stronger. 'Throw sand from the East to distract him.' The knight came forward ready for the sacrifice. The wind hissed, louder and louder. 'Blow, blow, blow. He cannot see. He is blind now. Make him lean away from the wind so he is easier to knock down.'

'Check,' I said, as the wind roared with laughter. The wind died down to little puffs, my own breath.

My mother placed my first trophy next to a new plastic chess set that the neighborhood Tao society had given to me. As she wiped each piece with a soft cloth, she said, 'Next time win more, lose less.'

'Ma, it's not how many pieces you lose,' I said. 'Sometimes you need to lose pieces to get ahead.'

'Better to lose less, see if you really need.'

At the next tournament, I won again, but it was my mother who wore the triumphant grin.

'Lost eight piece this time. Last time was eleven. What I tell you? Better off lose less!' I was annoyed, but I couldn't say anything.

I attended more tournaments, each one farther away from home. I won all games, in all divisions. The Chinese bakery downstairs from our flat displayed my growing collection of trophies in its window, amidst the dust-covered cakes that were never picked up. The day after I won an important regional tournament, the window encased a fresh sheet cake with whipped-cream frosting and red script saying 'Congratulations, Waverly Jong, Chinatown Chess Champion.' Soon after that, a flower shop, headstone engraver and funeral parlor offered to sponsor me in national tournaments. That's when my mother decided I no longer had to do the dishes. Winston and Vincent had to do my chores.

'Why does she get to play and we do all the work,' complained Vincent.

'Is new American rules,' said my mother. 'Meimei play,

squeeze all her brains out for win chess. You play, worth squeeze towel.'

By my ninth birthday, I was a national chess champion. I was still some 429 points away from grand-master status, but I was touted as the Great American Hope, a child prodigy and a girl to boot. They ran a photo of me in *Life* magazine next to a quote in which Bobby Fischer said, 'There will never be a woman grand master. 'Your Move, Bobby,' said the caption.

The day they took the magazine picture I wore neatly plaited braids clipped with plastic barrettes trimmed with rhinestones. I was playing in a large high school auditorium that echoed with phlegmy coughs and the squeaky rubber knobs of chair legs sliding across freshly waxed wooden floors. Seated across from me was an American man, about the same age as Lau Po, maybe fifty. I remember that his sweaty brow seemed to weep at my every move. He wore a dark, malodorous suit. One of his pockets was stuffed with a great white kerchief on which he wiped his palm before sweeping his hand over the chosen chess piece with great flourish.

In my crisp pink-and-white dress with scratchy lace at the neck, one of two my mother had sewn for these special occasions, I would clasp my hands under my chin, the delicate points of my elbows poised lightly on the table in the manner my mother had shown me for posing for the press. I would swing my patent leather shoes back and forth like an impatient child riding on a school bus. Then

I would pause, suck in my lips, twirl my chosen piece in midair as if undecided, and then firmly plant it in its new threatening place, with a triumphant smile thrown back at my opponent for good measure.

I no longer played in the alley of Waverly Place. I never visited the playground where the pigeons and old men gathered. I went to school, then directly home to learn new chess secrets, cleverly concealed advantages, more escape routes.

But I found it difficult to concentrate at home. My mother had a habit of standing over me while I plotted out my games. I think she thought of herself as my protective ally. Her lips would be sealed tight, and after each move I made, a soft 'Hmmmmph' would escape from her nose.

'Ma, I can't practice when you stand there like that,' I said one day. She retreated to the kitchen and made loud noises with the pots and pans. When the crashing stopped I could see out of the corner of my eye that she was standing in the doorway. 'Hmmmph!' Only this one came out of her tight throat.

My parents made many concessions to allow me to practice. One time I complained that the bedroom I shared was so noisy that I couldn't think. Thereafter, my brothers slept in a bed in the living room facing the street. I said I couldn't finish my rice; my head didn't work right when my stomach was too full. I left the table with half-finished bowls and nobody complained. But there was one duty I couldn't avoid. I had to accompany my mother on Saturday market days when I had no tournament to play. My mother would proudly walk with me, visiting many shops, buying very little. 'This my daughter Wave-ly Jong,' she said to whoever looked her way.

One day after we left a shop I said under my breath, 'I wish you wouldn't do that, telling everybody I'm your daughter.' My mother stopped walking. Crowds of people with heavy bags pushed past us on the sidewalk, bumping into first one shoulder, then another.

'Aiii-ya. So shame be with mother?' She grasped my hand even tighter as she glared at me.

I looked down. 'It's not that, it's just so obvious. It's just so embarrassing.'

'Embarrass you be my daughter?' Her voice was cracking with anger.

'That's not what I meant. That's not what I said.'

'What you say?'

I knew it was a mistake to say anything more, but I heard my voice speaking, 'Why do you have to use me to show off? If you want to show off, then why don't you learn to play chess?'

My mother's eyes turned into dangerous black slits. She had no words for me, just sharp silence.

I felt the wind rushing around my hot ears. I jerked my mother's tight grasp and spun around, knocking into an old woman. Her bag of groceries spilled to the ground.

'Aii-ya! Stupid girl!' my mother and the woman cried. Oranges and tin cans careened down the sidewalk. As my

27

mother stooped to help the old woman pick up the escaping food, I took off.

I raced down the street, dashing between people, not looking back as my mother screamed shrilly, 'Meimei! Meimei!' I fled down an alley, past dark, curtained shops and merchants washing the grime off their windows. I sped into the sunlight, into a large street crowded with tourists examining trinkets and souvenirs. I ducked into another dark alley, down another street, up another alley. I ran until it hurt and I realized I had nowhere to go, that I was not running from anything. The alleys contained no escape routes.

My breath came out like angry smoke. It was cold. I sat down on an upturned plastic pail next to a stack of empty boxes, cupping my chin with my hands, thinking hard. I imagined my mother, first walking briskly down one street or another looking for me, then giving up and returning home to await my arrival. After two hours, I stood up on creaking legs and slowly walked home.

The alley was quiet and I could see the yellow lights shining from our flat like two tiger's eyes in the night. I climbed the sixteen steps to the door, advancing quietly up each so as not to make any warning sounds. I turned the knob; the door was locked. I heard a chair moving, quick steps, the locks turning – click! click! click! – and then the door opened.

'About time you got home,' said Vincent. 'Boy, are you in trouble.'

He slid back to the dinner table. On a platter were the remains of a large fish, its fleshy head still connected to bones swimming upstream in vain escape. Standing there waiting for my punishment, I heard my mother speak in a dry voice.

'We not concerning this girl. This girl not have concerning for us.'

Nobody looked at me. Bone chopsticks clinked against the inside of bowls being emptied into hungry mouths.

I walked into my room, closed the door, and lay down on my bed. The room was dark, the ceiling filled with shadows from the dinnertime lights of neighboring flats.

In my head, I saw a chessboard with sixty-four black and white squares. Opposite me was my opponent, two angry black slits. She wore a triumphant smile. 'Strongest wind cannot be seen,' she said.

Her black men advanced across the plane, slowly marching to each successive level as a single unit. My white pieces screamed as they scurried and fell off the board one by one. As her men drew closer to my edge, I felt myself growing light. I rose up into the air and flew out the window. Higher and higher, above the alley, over the tops of tiled roofs, where I was gathered up by the wind and pushed up toward the night sky until everything below me disappeared and I was alone.

I closed my eyes and pondered my next move.

The Wardrobe, the Old Man and Death

Julio Ramón Ribeyro

The wardrobe in my father's room was not simply another piece of furniture, but was a house within a house. Inherited from his family, it followed us, huge and embarrassing, in move after move, until it came to its final resting place in his bedroom in Miraflores.

It took up almost half the room, and practically reached the ceiling. Whenever my father was away, my brothers and I ventured inside it. It was a real baroque palace, full of curlicues, mouldings, cornices, medallions and columns, carved down to the last detail by a demented nineteenth-century cabinetmaker It was in three parts, each with its own characteristics. The left-hand side had a door as heavy as a house entrance. From its lock dangled an enormous key, which for us was in itself a protean toy, serving equally well as a gun, a sceptre or a blackjack. It was in this part that my father hung his suits and an English coat that he never wore. This was our obligatory point of entry to a universe smelling of cedar and mothballs. The central section was the one we liked most, because of all the different things it contained. At the bottom were four deep drawers. When my father died, each of us inherited one of them, and we established our authority over them just as jealously as our father had over the entire wardrobe. Above the drawers came a niche which held thirty or so favourite books. And the central

31

part was topped off with a high quadrangular door that was always kept locked. We never did find out what it contained: perhaps all those papers and photos one trails with one from childhood, taking care not to destroy them for fear of losing part of a life which in fact, we have already lost. And finally, the right-hand side was another door, but this time faced with a bevelled mirror. It too had drawers at the bottom for shirts and underwear, and above it was an open space where a person could stand upright.

The left-hand side communicated with the right thanks to a passageway at the top, behind the book niche. This meant that one of our favourite games was to disappear inside the wardrobe through the heavy wooden door and pop out again a few seconds later from the door with the mirror. The top passage was also the perfect place to hide in hide-and-seek. Whenever we did, none of our friends could ever find us. Even though they knew we were in the wardrobe, they could never imagine we had clambered up it and were lying stretched out in the middle part as if in a coffin.

My father's bed was placed exactly opposite the right-hand section of the wardrobe, so that when he propped himself up on his pillows to read the newspaper, he could see himself in the mirror. He would look at himself in it, but even more than that, he would look at all those who had seen themselves in it before him. He would say: 'That's where don Juan Antonio Ribeyro y Estada looked at himself as he tied his bow tie before leaving for a ministerial meeting,' or 'That's where don Ramon Ribeyro y Alvarez del Villar would look at himself, before he left to give his lectures at San Marcos University,' or 'How many times I saw my father, don Julio Ribeyro y Benites look at himself in it when he was getting ready to go to Congress to make a speech.' His ancestors were all caught in the depths of the mirror. He could see them, and see his own image superimposed on theirs, in the unreal space, as if for once, by some miracle, they could all inhabit the same time together. Thanks to the mirror, my father entered the world of the dead, but he also used it to bring his ancestors into the world of the living.

We marvelled at the subtle ways that summer had of expressing itself, its endless fine days offering themselves for our pleasure, games and happiness. It even mellowed my father, who since his marriage had stopped drinking, smoking and seeing his friends: when he realized that the fruit trees in the small orchard had produced in abundance and invited admiration, and that we had finally purchased a proper set of china, he decided to occasionally throw his house open to one or other of his former companions.

The first of these was Alberto Rikets. He was the exact likeness of my father, but in miniature. Nature had taken the trouble to edit the copy, just in case. The two were equally pale, equally scrawny, and not only had the same gestures but the same turns of phrase. All this was due to the fact that they had studied in the same school, read the same books, spent similar sleepless nights, and suffered the same lengthy, painful illness. In the ten or twelve years since they had last seen each other, Rikets had made a fortune working all hours in a pharmacy, which now belonged to him, unlike father, who had barely managed to buy the house in Miraflores.

During those ten or twelve years, Rikets had achieved something else too: he had had a child, Alberto junior, whom he brought with him on the inaugural visit. Since the children of friends rarely get to be real friends themselves, we were suspicious of young Alberto at first. We thought he was skinny, clumsy and at times plain dumb. While my father was showing Alberto round his orchard, pointing out the orange tree, the fig, the apple tree and the vines, we took his son to play with us in our room. Alberto junior had no brothers or sisters, so he knew none of the games we invented and played together: he was no good as a Red Indian, and even worse at allowing himself to be plugged with bullets by the sheriff. None of us were convinced by the way he fell dead, and he could not understand that a tennis-racket could also be a machine-gun. We quickly decided it would be no good playing our favourite game in the wardrobe with him, so instead we concentrated on simple, repetitive pastimes, which left each of us to our own devices, like pushing toy cars across the floor, or building castles with wooden blocks.

While we were playing before lunch was called, we could see my father and his friend out of the window. By now, they were doing the rounds of the garden, because it was time to show off the magnolia, the geraniums, dahlias, carnations and wallflowers. My father had discovered the delights of gardening some years earlier, and the profound truth that was concealed in the shape of a sunflower or a rose bloom. That was why he spent his free days not as he had done previously, in wearisome readings that led him to reflect on the meaning of life, but in simple tasks such as watering, pruning, grafting or weeding, in all of which he invested a real intellectual passion. His love of books had been transferred wholesale on to his plants and flowers. He had created the entire garden, and like a character from Voltaire had concluded that his happiness came from tending it.

'One of these days I'm going to buy myself some land in Tarma, but not a tiny plot like this, no, a real farm: and *then* Alberto, you'll see what I'm truly capable of,' we heard our father say.

'My dear Perico, what about Chaclacayo instead of Tarma?' his friend said, referring to the luxury home he was having built there. 'The climate's almost as good, but it's only forty kilometres from Lima.'

'Yes, but my father lived in Tarma, not in Chaclacayo.'

There he was with his ancestors again! And the friends from his younger days called him Perico!

Alberto junior sent his car underneath the bed, crawled in to fetch it back, and we heard his shout of triumph. He had discovered a football under there. We'd been having such a hard time trying to keep him amused, and it was only now we found out that if he had a secret passion, the vice of a squalid, lonely kid, it was to kick a leather football around.

He had already grabbed it by the laces and was about to kick it, but we stopped him. It was madness to play in our room; in the garden it was strictly forbidden; so there was nothing else for it but to head out into the street.

That street had been the scene of dramatic games we had played years earlier against the Gómez brothers, games that lasted four or five hours and didn't end until it was completely dark, by which time we could no longer see either the goals or our opponents, and the games became a spectral struggle, a fierce, blind battle in which all kinds of cheating, fouls and unfair play took place. No professional team ever put so much hatred, such passionate determination, or pride into their games as we did in those childish encounters. That was why after the Gómez family moved away, we gave up football for good: nothing could ever rival those epic battles, so we hid the ball under our bed. Until Alberto junior went and found it. If it was football he wanted, we'd give him a bellyful of it.

We made the goal against the wall of our house so that the ball would bounce back. We stuck Alberto junior in goal. He saved our first efforts bravely enough. But then we really started bombarding him with vicious shots just so we'd have the pleasure of seeing him sprawling on the ground, spreadeagled and beaten.

Then it was his turn to shoot and I was in goal. For a

weakling, he had the kick of a mule, and though I stopped his first shot, the palms of my hands were stinging afterwards. His second shot was a perfect goal in the corner, but it was the third one that was the real beauty: the ball flashed through my hands, flew over the wall, sneaked through the branches of a climbing jasmine and over a cypress hedge, bounced on the trunk of the acacia tree and vanished into the depths of the house.

We sat on the pavement waiting for the maid to bring us back the ball, as usually happened. But nobody appeared. Just as we were getting up to go and look for it, the back door to the house opened, and my father came out, the ball under his arm. He was paler than ever. He didn't say a word to us, but strode over to the far side of the street and went up to a workman who was walking towards him whistling. When my father reached him, he put the ball in his hands and went back inside the house without even deigning to glance in our direction. It took the workman a moment to realize he had just been given a ball, but when he did so, he ran off so quickly we had no chance of catching him.

My mother was waiting at the door to call us to lunch. She looked so upset we realized something terrible must have happened. She waved us inside the house with a sharp gesture. 'How could you have done that!' was all she said as we filed past her.

It was when we saw that one of the windows in my father's room, the only one without bars on it, was half-open that we began to suspect what might have happened: Alberto junior, with a master stroke neither he nor anybody else could ever repeat even if they spent their whole lives trying, had managed to send the ball in an incredible arc that, in spite of walls, trees and bars, had hit the wardrobe mirror dead centre.

Lunch was a painful affair. Unable to scold us in front of his guest, my father choked on his anger in a silence no one dared to break. It was only at the dessert course that he softened a little, and told a few stories that delighted everyone. Alberto took his cue from him, and the meal ended in laughter. But that was too late to erase the impression that not only the lunch, but the invitation, my father's good intentions of trying to take up with his old friends again – something that was never repeated – had all been a complete fiasco.

To our horror, the Rikets left soon after; we were terrified our father would take the opportunity to punish us. But the visit had tired him out, and he went off to sleep his siesta without a word to us.

When he woke up, he gathered us in his room. He looked refreshed and calm, propped up on his pillows. He had had the windows opened wide so that the afternoon light could stream in.

'Look,' he said, pointing to the wardrobe.

It was indeed a sorry sight. In losing the mirror, the wardrobe had lost all its life. Where the glass had been, now there was only a rectangle of dark wood, a gloomy gap which reflected nothing and said nothing. It was like a shimmering lake whose waters had suddenly evaporated.

'The mirror my ancestors saw themselves in!' my father sighed, and dismissed us with a wave.

From that day on, we never again heard him mention his ancestors. In disappearing, the mirror had caused them to disappear too. My father was no longer tormented by his past; instead he peered with increasing curiosity into his future. Perhaps that was because he knew he hadn't long to live, and so no longer needed the mirror to get reunited with his forefathers – not in another life, he was not a believer – but in that world which captivated him just as books and flowers had before then: the world of nothingness.

Translated by Nick Caistor

Big Bill

Satyajit Ray

By Tulsi Babu's desk in his office on the ninth floor of a
building in Old Court House Street there is a window
which opens onto a vast expanse of the western sky. Tulsi
Babu's neighbour Jaganmoy Dutt had just gone to spit betel
juice out of the window one morning in the rainy season
when he noticed a double rainbow in the sky. He uttered
an exclamation of surprise and turned to Tulsi Babu.
'Come here, sir. You won't see the like of it every day.'

Tulsi Babu left his desk, went to his window, and looked
out.

'What are you referring to?' he asked.

'Why, the double rainbow!' said Jaganmoy Dutt. 'Are
you colour-blind?'

Tulsi Babu went back to his desk. 'I can't see what is so
special about a double rainbow. Even if there were twenty
rainbows in the sky, there would be nothing surprising
about that. Why, one can just as well go and stare at the
double-spired church in Lower Circular Road!'

Not everyone is endowed with the same sense of
wonder, but there is good reason to doubt whether Tulsi
Babu possesses any at all. There is only one thing that
never ceases to surprise him, and that is the excellence of
the mutton *kebab* at Mansur's. The only person who is
aware of this is Tulsi Babu's friend and colleague, Prodyot
Chanda.

Being of such a sceptical temperament, Tulsi Babu was not particularly surprised to find an unusually large egg while looking for medicinal plants in the forests of Dandakaranya.

Tulsi Babu had been dabbling in herbal medicine for the last fifteen years; his father was a well-known herbalist. Tulsi Babu's main source of income is as an upper division clerk in Arbuthnot & Co but he has not been able to discard the family profession altogether. Of late he has been devoting a little more time to it because two fairly distinguished citizens of Calcutta have benefited from his prescriptions, thus giving a boost to his reputation as a part-time herbalist.

It was herbs again which had brought him to Dandakaranya. He had heard that thirty miles to the north of Jagdalpur there lived a holy man in a mountain cave who had access to some medicinal plants including one for high blood pressure which was even more efficacious than *rawolfa serpentina*. Tulsi Babu suffered from hypertension; *serpentina* hadn't worked too well in his case, and he had no faith in homeopathy or allopathy.

Tulsi Babu had taken his friend Prodyot Babu with him on this trip to Jagdalpur. Tulsi Babu's inability to feel surprise had often bothered Prodyot Babu. One day he was forced to comment, 'All one needs to feel a sense of wonder is a little imagination. You are so devoid of it that even if a full-fledged ghost were to appear before you, you wouldn't be surprised.' Tulsi Babu had replied calmly, 'To feign surprise when one doesn't actually feel it, is an affectation. I do not approve of it.'

But this didn't get in the way of their friendship.

The two checked into a hotel in Jagdalpur during the autumn vacation. On the way, in the Madras Mail, two foreign youngsters had got into their compartment. They turned out to be Swedes. One of them was so tall that his head nearly touched the ceiling. Prodyot Babu had asked him how tall he was and the young man had replied, 'Two metres and seven centimetres.' Which is nearly seven feet. Prodyot Babu couldn't take his eyes away from this young giant during the rest of the journey; and yet Tulsi Babu was not surprised. He said such extraordinary height was simply the result of the diet of the Swedish people, and therefore nothing to be surprised at.

They reached the cave of the holy man Dhumai Baba after walking through the forest for a mile or so then climbing up about five hundred feet. The cave was a large one, but since no sun ever reached it, they only had to take ten steps to be engulfed in darkness, thickened by the ever present smoke from the Baba's brazier. Prodyot Babu was absorbed in watching, by the light of his torch, the profusion of stalactites and stalagmites while Tulsi Babu inquired after his herbal medicine. The tree that Dhumai Baba referred to was known as *chakraparna*, which is the Sanskrit for 'round leaves'. Tulsi Babu had never heard of it, nor was it mentioned in any of the half-dozen books he had read on herbal medicine. It was not a tree, but a shrub.

It was found only in one part of the forest of Dandakaranya, and nowhere else. Baba gave adequate directions which Tulsi Babu noted down carefully.

Coming out of the cave, Tulsi Babu lost no time in setting off in quest of the herb. Prodyot Babu was happy to keep his friend company; he had hunted big game at one time – conservation had put an end to that, but the lure of the jungle persisted.

The holy man's directions proved accurate. Half an hour's walk brought them to a ravine which they crossed and in three minutes they found the shrub seven steps to the south of a *neem* tree scorched by lightning – a waist-high shrub with round green leaves, each with a pink dot in the centre.

'What kind of a place is this?' asked Prodyot Babu, looking around.

'Why, what's wrong with it?'

'But for the *neem*, there isn't a single tree here that I know. And see how damp it is. Quite unlike the places we've passed through.'

It *was* moist underfoot, but Tulsi Babu saw nothing strange in that. Why, in Calcutta itself, the temperature varied between one neighbourhood and another. Tollygunge in the south was much cooler than Shambazar in the north. What was so strange about one part of a forest being different from another? It was nothing but a quirk of nature.

Tulsi Babu had just put the bag down on the ground and

stooped towards the shrub when a sharp query from Prodyot Babu interrupted him.

'What on earth is that?'

Tulsi Babu had seen the thing too, but was not bothered by it. 'Must be some sort of egg,' he said.

Prodyot Babu had thought it was a piece of egg-shaped rock, but on getting closer he realised that it was a genuine egg, yellow, with brown stripes flecked with blue. What could such a large egg belong to? A python?

Meanwhile, Tulsi Babu had already plucked some leafy branches off the shrub and put them in his bag. He wanted to take some more but something happened then which made him stop.

The egg chose this very moment to hatch. Prodyot Babu had jumped back at the sound of the cracking shell, but now he took courage to take a few steps towards it.

The head was already out of the shell. Not a snake, nor a croc or a turtle, but a bird.

Soon the whole creature was out. It stood on spindly legs and looked around. It was quite large; about the size of a hen. Prodyot Babu was very fond of birds and kept a mynah and a bulbul as pets; but he had never seen a chick as large as this, with such a large beak and long legs. Its purple plumes were unique, as was its alert behaviour so soon after birth.

Tulsi Babu, however, was not in the least interested in the chick. He had been intent on stuffing his bag with as much of the herb as would go into it.

Prodyot Babu looked around and commented, 'Very surprising; there seems to be no sign of its parents, at least not in the vicinity.'

'I think that's enough surprise for a day,' said Tulsi Babu, hoisting his bag on his shoulder. 'It's almost four. We must be out of the forest before it gets dark.'

Somewhat against his wish, Prodyot Babu turned away from the chick and started walking with Tulsi Babu. It would take at least half an hour to reach the waiting taxi.

A patter of feet made Prodyot Babu stop and turn round. The chick was following them.

'I say –' called out Prodyot Babu.

Tulsi Babu now stopped and turned. The chick was looking straight at him. Then it padded across and stopped in front of Tulsi Babu where it opened its unusually large beak and gripped the edge of Tulsi Babu's dhoti.

Prodyot Babu was so surprised that he didn't know what to say, until he saw Tulsi Babu pick up the chick and shove it into his bag. 'What d'you think you're doing?' he cried in consternation. 'You put that nameless chick in your bag?'

'I've always wanted to keep a pet,' said Tulsi Babu, resuming his walk. 'Even mongrels are kept as pets. What's wrong with a nameless chick?'

Prodyot Babu saw the chick sticking its neck out of the swinging bag and glancing around with wide-open eyes.

Tulsi Babu lived in a flat on the second floor of a building in Masjidbari Street. Besides Tulsi Babu, who was a

46

bachelor, there was his servant Natobar and his cook Joykesto. There was another flat on the same floor, and this was occupied by Tarit Sanyal, the proprietor of the Nabarun Press. Mr Sanyal was a short-tempered man made even more so by repeated power failures in the city which seriously affected the working of his press.

Two months had passed since Tulsi Babu's return from Dandakaranya. He had put the chick in a cage which he had specially ordered immediately upon his return. The cage was kept in a corner of the inner veranda. He had found a Sanskrit name for the chick: *Bribat-Chanchu*, or Big Bill; soon the Big was dropped and now it was just Bill.

The very first day he had acquired the chick in Jagdalpur, Tulsi Babu had tried to feed it grain. The chick had refused. Tulsi Babu had guessed, and rightly, that it was probably a meat eater; ever since he has been feeding it insects. Of late the bird's appetite seems to have grown, and Tulsi Babu has been obliged to feed it meat; Natobar buys meat from the market regularly, which may explain the bird's rapid growth in size.

Tulsi Babu had been far-sighted enough to buy a cage which was several sizes too large for the bird. His instinct had told him that the bird belonged to a large species. The roof of the cage was two and a half feet from the ground, but only yesterday Tulsi Babu had noticed that when Bill stood straight its head nearly touched the roof; even though the bird was only two months old, it would soon need a larger cage.

Nothing has so far been said about the cry of the bird,

47

which made Mr Sanyal choke on his tea one morning while he stood on the veranda. Normally the two neighbours hardly spoke to each other; today, after he had got over his fit of coughing, Mr Sanyal demanded to know what kind of an animal Tulsi Babu kept in his cage that yelled like that. It was true that the cry was more beast-like than bird-like.

Tulsi Babu was getting dressed to go to work. He appeared at the bedroom door and said, 'Not an animal, but a bird. And whatever its cry, it certainly doesn't keep one awake at night the way your cat does.'

Tulsi Babu's retort put an end to the argument, but Mr Sanyal kept grumbling. It was a good thing the cage couldn't be seen from his flat; a sight of the bird might have given rise to even more serious consequences.

Although its looks didn't bother Tulsi Babu, they certainly worried Prodyot Babu. The two met rarely outside office hours, except once a week for a meal of *kebab* and *paratha* at Mansur's. Prodyot Babu had a large family and many responsibilities. But since the visit to Dandakaranya, Tulsi Babu's pet was often on his mind. As a result he had started to drop in at Tulsi Babu's from time to time in the evenings. The bird's astonishing rate of growth and the change in its appearance were a constant source of surprise to Prodyot Babu. He was at a loss to see why Tulsi Babu should show no concern about it. Prodyot Babu had never imagined that the look in a bird's eye could be so malevolent. The black pupils in the amber irises would fix Prodyot Babu with such an unwavering look that he

48

would feel most uneasy. The bird's beak naturally grew as well as its body; shiny black in colour, it resembled an eagle's beak but was much larger in relation to the rest of the body. It was clear, from its rudimentary wings and its long sturdy legs and sharp talons, that the bird couldn't fly. Prodyot Babu had described the bird to many acquaintances, but no one had been able to identify it.

One Sunday Prodyot Babu came to Tulsi Babu with a camera borrowed from a nephew. There wasn't enough light in the cage, so he had come armed with a flash gun. Photography had been a hobby with him once, and he was able to summon up enough courage to point the camera at the bird in the cage and press the shutter. The scream of protest from the bird as the flash went off sent Prodyot Babu reeling back a full yard, and it struck him that the bird's cry should be recorded; showing the photograph and playing back the cry might help in the identification of the species. Something rankled in Prodyot Babu's mind; he hadn't yet mentioned it to Tulsi Babu but somewhere in a book or a magazine he had seen a picture of a bird which greatly resembled this pet of Tulsi Babu's. If he came across the picture again, he would compare it with the photograph.

When the two friends were having tea, Tulsi Babu came out with a new piece of information. Ever since Bill had arrived, crows and sparrows had stopped coming to the flat. This was a blessing because the sparrows would build nests in the most unlikely places, while the crows would make off with food from the kitchen. All that had stopped.

'Is that so?' asked Prodyot Babu, surprised as usual.

'Well, you've been here all this time; have you seen any other birds?'

Prodyot Babu realised that he hadn't. 'But what about your two servants? Have they got used to Bill?'

'The cook never goes near the cage, but Natobar feeds it meat with pincers. Even if he does have any objection, he hasn't come out with it. And when the bird turns nasty, one sight of me calms it down. By the way, what was the idea behind taking the photograph?'

Prodyot Babu didn't mention the real reason. He said, 'When it's no more, it'll remind you of it.'

Prodyot Babu had the photograph developed and printed the following day. He also had two enlargements made. One he gave to Tulsi Babu and the other he took to the ornithologist Ranajoy Shome. Only the other day an article by Mr Shome on the birds of Sikkim had appeared in the weekly magazine *Desh*.

But Mr Shome failed to identify the bird from the photograph. He asked where the bird could be seen, and Prodyot Babu answered with a bare-faced lie. 'A friend of mine has sent this photograph from Osaka. He wanted me to identify the bird for him.'

Tulsi Babu noted the date in his diary: February the fourteenth, 1980. Big Bill, who had been transferred from a three-and-a-half-foot cage to a four-and-a-half-foot one only last month, had been guilty of a misdeed last night.

Tulsi Babu had been awakened by a suspicious sound in

the middle of the night. A series of hard, metallic twangs. But the sound had soon stopped and had been followed by total silence.

Still, the suspicion that something was up lingered in Tulsi Babu's mind. He came out of the mosquito net. Moonlight fell on the floor through the grilled window. Tulsi Babu put on his slippers, took the electric torch from the table, and came out on to the veranda.

In the beam of the torch he saw that the meshing on the cage had been ripped apart and a hole large enough for the bird to escape from had been made. The cage was now empty.

Tulsi Babu's torch revealed nothing on this side of the veranda. At the opposite end, the veranda turned right towards Mr Sanyal's flat.

Tulsi Babu reached the corner in a flash and swung his torch to the right.

It was just as he feared.

Mr Sanyal's cat was now a helpless captive in Bill's beak. The shiny spots on the floor were obviously drops of blood. But the cat was still alive and thrashing its legs about.

Tulsi Babu now cried out 'Bill' and the bird promptly dropped the cat from its beak.

Then it advanced with long strides, turned the corner, and went quietly back to its cage.

Even in this moment of crisis, Tulsi Babu couldn't help heaving a sigh of relief.

A padlock hung on the door of Mr Sanyal's room; Mr

Sanyal had left three days ago for a holiday, after the busy months of December and January when school books were printed in his press.

The best thing to do with the cat would be to toss it out of the window on to the street. Stray cats and dogs were run over every day on the streets of Calcutta; this would be just one more of them.

The rest of the night Tulsi Babu couldn't sleep.

The next day Tulsi Babu had to absent himself from work for an hour or so while he went to the railway booking office; he happened to know one of the booking clerks which made his task easier. Prodyot Babu had asked after the bird and Tulsi Babu had replied he was fine. Then he had added after a brief reflection – 'I'm thinking of framing the photo you took of it.'

On the twenty-fourth of February, Tulsi Babu arrived in Jagdalpur for the second time. A packing case with Bill in it arrived in the luggage van in the same train. The case was provided with a hole for ventilation.

From Jagdalpur, Tulsi Babu set off in a luggage caravan with two coolies and the case for the precise spot in the forest where he had found the bird.

At a certain milepost on the main road, Tulsi Babu got off the vehicle and, with the coolies carrying the packing case, set off for the scorched *neem* tree. It took nearly an hour to reach the spot. The coolies put the case down. They had already been generously tipped and told that they would have to open the packing case. This was done, and Tulsi Babu was relieved to see that Bill was in fine fettle. The coolies, of course, bolted screaming at the sight of the bird, but that didn't worry Tulsi Babu. His purpose had been served. Bill was looking at him with a fixed stare. Its head already touched the four-and-a-half-foot high roof of the cage.

'Good-bye, Bill.'

The sooner the parting took place the better.

Tulsi Babu started his journey back to the Tempo.

Tulsi Babu hadn't told anybody in the office about his trip, not even Prodyot Babu, who naturally asked where he had been when he appeared at his desk on Monday. Tulsi Babu replied briefly that he had been to a niece's wedding in Naihati.

About a fortnight later, on a visit to Tulsi Babu's place, Prodyot Babu was surprised to see the cage empty. He asked about the bird. 'It's gone,' said Tulsi Babu.

Prodyot Babu naturally assumed that the bird was dead. He felt a twinge of remorse. He hadn't meant it seriously when he had said that the photo would remind Tulsi Babu of his pet when it was no more; he had no idea the bird would die so soon. The photograph he had taken had been framed and was hanging on the wall of the bedroom. Tulsi Babu seemed out of sorts; altogether the atmosphere was gloomy. To relieve the gloom, Prodyot Babu made a suggestion. 'We haven't been to Mansur's in long while. What about going tonight for a meal of *kebab* and *paratha?*'

'I'm afraid I have quite lost my taste for them.'

Prodyot Babu couldn't believe his ears. 'Lost your taste

for *kebabs?* What's the matter? Aren't you well? Have you tried the herb the holy man prescribed?'

Tulsi Babu said that his blood pressure had come down to normal since he tried the juice of the *chakra-parna.* What he didn't bother to mention was that he had forgotten all about herbal medicines as long as Bill had been with him, and that he had gone back to them only a week ago.

'By the way,' remarked Prodyot Babu, 'the mention of the herb reminds me – did you read in the papers today about the forest of Dandakaranya?'

'What did the papers say?'

Tulsi Babu bought a daily newspaper all right, but rarely got beyond the first page. The paper was near at hand. Prodyot Babu pointed out the news to him. The headline said 'The Terror of Dandakaranya'.

The news described a sudden and unexpected threat to the domestic animals and poultry in the villages around the forests of Dandakaranya. Some unknown species of animal had started to devour them. No tigers are known to exist in that area, and proof has been found that something other than a feline species had been causing the havoc. Tigers usually drag their prey to their lairs; this particular beast doesn't. The shikaris engaged by the Madhya Pradesh Government had searched for a week but failed to locate any beasts capable of such carnage. As a result, panic has spread amongst the villagers. One particular villager claims that he had seen a two-legged creature running away from his cowshed. He had gone to investigate, and found his buffalo lying dead with a sizeable portion of his lower abdomen eaten away.

Tulsi Babu read the news, folded the paper, and put it back on the table.

'Don't tell me you don't find anything exceptional in the story?' said Prodyot Babu.

Tulsi Babu shook his head. In other words, he didn't.

Three days later a strange thing happened to Prodyot Babu.

At breakfast, his wife opened a tin of Digestive biscuits and served them to her husband with his tea.

The next moment Prodyot Babu had left the dining-table and rushed out of the house.

By the time he reached his friend Animesh's flat in Ekdalia Road, he was trembling with excitement.

He snatched the newspaper away from his friend's hands, threw it aside and said panting: 'Where d'you keep your copies of *Readers' Digest*? Quick – it's most important!'

Animesh shared with millions of others a taste for *Readers' Digest*. He was greatly surprised by his friend's behaviour but scarcely had the opportunity to show it. He went to a bookcase and dragged out some dozen issues of the magazine from the bottom shelf.

'Which number are you looking for?'

Prodyot Babu took the whole bunch, flipped through the pages issue after issue, and finally found what he was looking for.

'Yes – this is the bird. No doubt about it.'

His fingers rested on a picture of a conjectural model of a bird kept in the Chicago Museum of Natural History. It showed an attendant cleaning the model with a brush.

'*Andalgalornis*,' said Prodyot Babu, reading out the name. The name meant terror-bird. A huge prehistoric species, carnivorous, faster than a horse, and extremely ferocious.

The doubt which had crept into Prodyot Babu's mind was proved right when in the office next morning Tulsi Babu came to him and said that he had to go to Dandakaranya once again, and that he would be delighted if Prodyot Babu would join him and bring his gun with him. There was too little time to obtain sleeping accommodation in the train, but that couldn't be helped as the matter was very urgent.

Prodyot Babu agreed at once.

In the excitement of the pursuit, the two friends didn't mind the discomfort of the journey. Prodyot Babu said nothing about the bird in the *Readers' Digest*. He could do so later; there was plenty of time for that. Tulsi Babu had in the meantime told everything to Prodyot Babu. He had also mentioned that he didn't really believe the gun would be needed; he had suggested taking it only as a precaution. Prodyot Babu, on the other hand, couldn't share his friend's optimism. He believed the gun was essential, and he was fully prepared for any eventuality. Today's paper had mentioned that the Madhya Pradesh Government had announced a reward of 5,000 rupees to anyone who succeeded in killing or capturing the

56

creature, which had been declared a man-eater ever since a woodcutter's son had fallen victim to it.

In Jagdalpur, permission to shoot the creature was obtained from the conservator of forests, Mr Tirumalai. But he warned that Tulsi Babu and Prodyot Babu would have to go on their own as nobody could be persuaded to go into the forest any more.

Prodyot Babu asked if any information had been received from the shikaris who had preceded them. Tirumalai turned grave. 'So far four shikaris have attempted to kill the beast. Three of them had no success. The fourth never returned.'

'Never returned?'

'No. Ever since then shikaris have been refusing to go. So you had better think twice before undertaking the trip.'

Prodyot Babu was shaken, but his friend's nonchalance brought back his courage. 'I think we will go,' he said.

This time they had to walk a little further because the taxi refused to take the dirt road which went part of the way into the forest. Tulsi Babu was confident that the job would be over in two hours, and the taxi agreed to wait that long upon being given a tip of fifty rupees. The two friends set off on their quest.

It being springtime now, the forest wore a different look from the previous trips. Nature was following its course, and yet there was an unnatural silence. There were no bird calls; not even the cries of cuckoos.

As usual, Tulsi Babu was carrying his shoulder bag. Prodyot Babu knew there was a packet in it, but he didn't know what it contained. Prodyot Babu himself was carrying his rifle and bullets.

As the undergrowth was thinner they could see farther into the forest. That is why the two friends were able to see from a distance the body of a man lying spread-eagled on the ground behind a jackfruit tree. Tulsi Babu hadn't noticed it, and stopped only when Prodyot Babu pointed it out to him. Prodyot Babu took a firm grip on the gun and walked towards the body. Tulsi Babu seemed only vaguely interested in the matter.

Prodyot Babu went halfway, and then turned back.

'You look as if you've seen a ghost,' said Tulsi Babu when his friend rejoined him. 'Isn't that the missing shikari?'

'It must be,' said Prodyot Babu hoarsely. 'But it won't be easy to identify the corpse. The head's missing.'

The rest of the way they didn't speak at all.

It took one hour to reach the *neem* tree, which meant they must have walked at least three miles. Prodyot Babu noticed that the medicinal shrub had grown fresh leaves and was back to its old shape.

'Bill! Billie!'

There was something faintly comic about the call, and Prodyot Babu couldn't help smiling. But the next moment he realised that for Tulsi Babu the call was quite natural. That he had succeeded in taming the monster bird, Prodyot Babu had seen with his own eyes.

Tulsi Babu's call resounded in the forest.

'Bill! Bill! Billie!'

Now Prodyot Babu saw something stirring in the depths

58

of the forest. It was coming towards them, and at such a speed that it seemed to grow bigger and bigger every second.

It was the monster bird.

The gun in Prodyot Babu's hand suddenly felt very heavy. He wondered if he would be able to use it at all.

The bird slowed down and approached them stealthily through the vegetation.

Andalgalornis. Prodyot Babu would never forget the name. A bird as tall as a man. Ostriches were tall too; but that was largely because of their neck. This bird's back itself was as high as an average man. In other words, the bird had grown a foot and a half in just about a month. The colour of its plumes had changed too. There were blotches of black on the purple. And the malevolent look in its amber eyes which Prodyot Babu found he could confront when the bird was in captivity, was now for him unbearably terrifying. The look was directed at its ex-master.

There was no knowing what the bird would do. Thinking its stillness to be a prelude to an attack, Prodyot Babu had made an attempt to raise the gun with his shaking hands. But the moment he did so, the bird turned its gaze at him, its feathers puffing out to give it an even more terrifying appearance.

'Lower the gun,' hissed Tulsi Babu in a tone of admonition.

Prodyot Babu obeyed. Now the bird lowered its feathers too and transferred its gaze to its master.

'I don't know if you are still hungry,' said Tulsi Babu, 'but I hope you will eat this because I am giving it to you.'

Tulsi Babu had already brought out the packet from the bag. He now unwrapped it and tossed the contents towards the bird. It was a large chunk of meat.

'You've been the cause of my shame. I hope you will behave yourself from now on.'

Prodyot Babu saw that the bird picked up the chunk with its huge beak, and proceeded to masticate it.

'This time it really is good-bye.'

Tulsi Babu turned. Prodyot Babu was afraid to turn his back on the bird, and for a while walked backwards with his eyes on the bird. When he found that the bird was making no attempt to follow him or attack him, he too turned round and joined his friend.

A week later the news came out in the papers of the end of the terror in Dandakaranya. Prodyot Babu had not mentioned anything to Tulsi Babu about *Andalgalornis*, and the fact that the bird had been extinct for three million years. But the news in the papers today obliged him to come to his friend. 'I'm at a loss to know how it happened,' he said. 'Perhaps you may throw some light on it.'

'There's no mystery at all,' said Tulsi Babu. 'I only mixed some of my medicine with the meat I gave him.'

Medicine?'

'An extract of *chakra-parna*. It turns one into a vegetarian. Just as it has done me.'

The Liar

Mulk Raj Anand

Labhu, the old Shikari of my village, was a born liar. Therefore he had won the reputation of being the best storyteller in our parts. And though a sweeper of low caste, he was honoured by all and sundry. He was tolerated even to the extent of being given a seat at the foot of the banyan tree. And my mother did not insist too harshly on the necessity of my taking a bath to purify myself every time I had been seen listening to one of his uncanny tales with the other village boys.

Labhu was a thin, little man, with the glint of a lance and the glide of an arrow. His wiry, weather-beaten frame must have had immense reserves of energy, to judge by the way he could chase stags up the steep crags of the hills behind our village and run abreast of the bay mare of Subedar Deep Singh to whose household he was attached as a Shikari, except when some English official, a rich white merchant, or a guest of the Subedar, engaged him for a season. It was perhaps this wonderful physical agility of his that had persuaded him to adopt the profession of a Shikari. Labhu had also a sensitive, dark face of which the lower lip trembled as it pronounced the first accents of a poignant verse or the last words of a gruesome hunting story. And it was the strange spell that his tragic verses and weird stories cast on me that made me his devoted follower through childhood. He taught me

61

the way to track all the wild animals; and he taught me how to concoct a cock-and-bull story to tell my father if I had to make an excuse for not being at home during the reign of the hot sun.

His teaching was, of course, by example, as I was rather a critical pupil.

'Labhu,' I would say, 'I am sure it is impossible to track any prey when you are half up the side of a hillock.'

'*Achha*,' he would say, 'I will show you. Stand still and listen.' I did so and we both heard a pebble drop. Up he darted on the stony ridge in the direction whence the sound had come, jumping from crag to crag, securing a precarious foothold on a small stone here and a sure one on a boulder there, till he was tearing through a flock of sheep, towards a little gully where a ram had taken shelter in a cave, secure in the belief that it would escape its pursuer.

'All right,' I would say. 'You may have been able to track this ram, but I don't believe that yarn of yours about the devil ram you saw when you were hunting with the Subedar.'

'I swear by God Almighty,' he said, 'it is true. The Subedar will tell you that he saw this terrible apparition with me. It was a beast about the size of an elephant, with eyes as big as hens' eggs and a beard as long as that of Maulvi Shah Din, the priest of the mosque, not only henna-dyed and red, but blue-black; it had huge ears as big as an elephant's, which did not flap, however, but pricked up like the ears of the Subedar's horse; it had a nose like that of the wife of the missionary Sahib, and it had square jaws which showed teeth almost as big as the chunks of marble which lie outside the temple, as it laughed at the Subedar. It appeared unexpectedly near the peak of Devi Parbat. The Subedar and I had ascended about twelve thousand feet up the mountain in search of game, when suddenly, out of the spirit world that always waits about us in the living air, there was the clattering of stones and boulders, the whistling of sharp winds, the gurgling of thunder and a huge crack on the side of the mountain. Then an enormous figure seemed to rise. From a distance it seemed to both of us like a dark patch, and we thought it was an *oorial* and began to stalk towards it. What was our surprise, however, when, as soon as we saw it stand there, facing us with its glistening, white eyes as a hen's egg, it sneezed and ripped the mountainside with a kick of its forefeet and disappeared. The mountain shook and the Subedar trembled, while I stood bravely where I was and laughed till I wept with joy at my good luck in having seen so marvellous a manifestation of the devil-god of the tribe of rams. I tell you, son, please God I shall show him to you one of these days.'

'Labhu, you don't mean to say so!' I said, half-incredulous, though I was fascinated by the chimaera.

'Of course I mean to say so, silly boy,' said Labhu. 'This is nothing compared to the other vision that was vouchsafed to me, praise be to God, when I was on the journey to Ladakh, hunting with Jolly John Sahib.' And he began to relate a fantastic story of a colossal snake, which was so improbable that even I did not believe it.

63

'Oh, you are a fool, Labhu,' I said. 'And you are a liar. Everybody says so. And I don't believe you at all. My mother says I am silly to believe your tales.'

'All right, then if you don't believe my stories why do you come here to listen to them?' he said, with wounded pride. 'Go, I shall never teach you anything more, and I shall certainly not let you accompany me to the hunts.'

'All right,' I said, chagrined and stubborn. 'I don't want to speak to you either.'

And I ran home bursting with indignation at having forced a quarrel upon Labhu, when really he only told me his stories for my amusement.

Labhu went away for a while on a hunting tour with the Subedar. He didn't come back to the village when this tour finished, because Subedar Deep Singh's eldest son, Kuldeep Singh, who was lieutenant in the army, took him for a trip across the Himalayas to Nepal.

During this time, though I regretted Labhu's absence, I lent my ear readily to the malicious misrepresentation of his character that the Subedar and his employers, and occasionally also my father, indulged in; because, though superior to Labhu by caste, they were not such good shots as he was.

'He can only wait by a forest pool or a safe footpath to shoot at some unfortunate beast, this Labhu!' said the Subedar. 'And often he shoots in the dark with that inefficient powdergun of his. He is no good except for tracking.'

'Yes,' said my father, 'he is a vain boaster and a liar. The

64

only beast he dared to shoot at while he was with me was a hare and even that he hit in the leg.'

I waited eagerly for Labhu's return to confirm from his very mouth these stories of his incompetence, because, though incredulous of this scandal, I had been driven to a frenzy of chagrin by his insulting dismissal of me. I thought I would ask him point-blank whether he was really as bad a hunter as the Subedar and my father made him out to be.

When Labhu came back however, he limped about and seemed ill. It was very sad to see him broken and dispirited. And I forgot all the scandal I had heard about him in my bafflement at the sudden change that had come into his character, for he was now no longer the garrulous man who sat telling stories to old men and young boys, but a strangely reticent creature who lay in a stupor all day, moaning and murmuring to himself in a prolonged delirium, except that he occasionally hobbled out with a huge staff in his hand in the evenings.

I was afraid to go near him, because he always wore a forbidding, angry look. But the villagers didn't seem to think there was anything the matter with Labhu, as I heard them say, 'Now that we have no patience with him and his stories, he spends most of his time telling them to himself, the fool!'

I owed a loyalty to Labhu, for I had discovered a kinship in my make-up for all those extravagances for which the Shikari was so well known.

So I went up to him one day, as he lay on a broken

string-bed near his mud hut, under the precarious shelter which a young pipal gave him.

'You have returned then, Master Labhu,' I said.

'Yes,' he said, 'I have been back some time, son. I looked for you, but you did not seem to be about. But you know, the man who is slain cannot walk even to his own house. This leg of mine pains me and I can't get about as I used to.'

'What happened to your leg, then?' I asked, realising that he had forgotten all about our past quarrels and was as kind and communicative to me as before. 'Did you fall down a cliff or something?'

'No,' he said in a tired voice. And he kept quiet for a long while.

'What happened then?' I persisted.

'You know, son,' Labhu began, at first pale and hesitant, then smiling and lifting his eyebrows in the familiar manner of the old days, 'I went away on a hunting tour in the pay of the Subedar's eldest son, Kuldeep Singh, and some of his friends. Well, we went to Nepal through the Kulu valley. They had no experience of hunting in this or in any other part of the world, and I led them across such trails as I knew and such as the local shikaris told me about. That boy, Kuldeep, I don't know what he does in the army, but he can't shoot at any range, and the Sahibs with him were clumsy, purblind white men. I would point to a beast with my stick, and, though they could see the hide before their eyes, they bungled with their guns or were too noisy on their feet, and away crashed the bull

66

which we had been tracking. I would grunt, shrug my shoulders and did not mind, because they were like children. They had finished hundreds of cartridges and had not shot anything, and daily begged me to help them to secure some game.

'At first I told them that game doesn't taste sweet unless it is shot by oneself. But at length I took pity on them and thought that I would secure them a good mixed bag. I shot twelve tigers with my gun and fifteen panthers in the course of seven days, and many stags.

'On the eighth day we saw a monster which had the body of a wild bear, the head of a reindeer, the feet of a goat, the tail of a wild bull and a glistening, fibrous tissue all round it like the white silken veil which the Rani of Boondi wore when she came to visit Subedar Deep Singh's wife. Kuldeep Singh and the Sahibs were very frightened of this apparition and said it was the devil himself who had the shape of an earthly being and who would soon breathe a breath which would mix with the still air of the night and poison life.

'They were all for killing it outright, while I was sure that it was only a princess of the royal house of Nepal who had been transformed by some magician into this fantastic shape and size. And I wanted to catch it alive and bring it home to be my bride.'

Labhu went on to relate how beautiful she was and how he resolved to restore her to her normal self by reading magical incantations.

'I told her I loved her,' he continued, 'and she smiled

shyly. But some fool, I think it was the Subedar's son, fired a volley of shots, which frightened her so that she ran, became one with the air and began to ascend the snowy peaks of Kailash Parbat.

'I was bent on rescuing my beloved, and I leaped from one mountain to another, calling after her to stop. But that idiot Kuldeep and the Sahibs kept on shooting and roused the magician who kept guard over her. And this evil sage threw a huge mountain of snow at me to kill me.

'I just blew a hot breath and the mountain of snow cracked into a million pieces and hung about the sky like glittering stars.

'Then the magician struck the earth with his feet and opened up a grave to bury me alive. I leapt right across the fissure and found myself on a peak in the land of the lama who never dies.

'By now, of course, the magician had hidden the beauty away in some cave. So, I gave up the chase, as there was the doom of death about his beauty, anyhow, and I made one leap across the Himalayas for home ...'

'And as you landed this side of the mountains you sprained your foot,' I said.

Labhu lifted his eyebrows funnily in the manner of the old days and, laughing, said: 'Have I told you this story before, then?'

To Build a Fire

Jack London

Day had broken cold and grey, exceedingly cold and grey, when the man turned aside from the main Yukon trail and climbed the high earth-bank, where a dim and little-travelled trail led eastward through the fat spruce timber-land. It was a steep bank, and he paused for breath at the top, excusing the act to himself by looking at his watch. It was nine o'clock. There was no sun nor hint of sun, though there was not a cloud in the sky. It was a clear day, and yet there seemed an intangible pall over the face of things, a subtle gloom that made the day dark, and that was due to the absence of sun. This fact did not worry the man. He was used to the lack of sun. It had been days since he had seen the sun, and he knew that a few more days must pass before that cheerful orb, due south, would just peep above the sky-line and dip immediately from view.

The man flung a look back along the way he had come. The Yukon lay a mile wide and hidden under three feet of ice. On top of this ice were as many feet of snow. It was all pure white, rolling in gentle undulations where the ice-jams of the freeze-up had formed. North and south, as far as his eye could see, it was unbroken white, save for a dark hair-line that curved and twisted from around the spruce-covered island to the south, and that curved and twisted away into the north, where it disappeared behind another spruce-covered island. This dark hair-line was the trail –

the main trail – that led south five hundred miles to the Chilcoot Pass, Dyea, and salt water; and that led north seventy miles to Dawson, and still on to the north a thousand miles to Nulato, and finally to St Michael on Bering Sea, a thousand miles and half a thousand more.

But all this – the mysterious, far-reaching hair-line trail, the absence of sun from the sky, the tremendous cold, and the strangeness and weirdness of it all – made no impression on the man. It was not because he was long used to it. He was a new-comer in the land, a *chechaquo*, and this was his first winter. The trouble with him was that he was without imagination. He was quick and alert in the things of life, but only in the things, and not in the significances. Fifty degrees below zero meant eighty-odd degrees of frost. Such fact impressed him as being cold and uncomfortable, and that was all. It did not lead him to meditate upon his frailty as a creature of temperature, and upon man's frailty in general, able only to live within certain narrow limits of heat and cold; and from there on it did not lead him to the conjectural field of immortality and man's place in the universe. Fifty degrees below zero stood for a bite of frost that hurt and that must be guarded against by the use of mittens, ear-flaps, warm moccasins, and thick socks. Fifty degrees below zero was to him just precisely fifty degrees below zero. That there should be anything more to it than that was a thought that never entered his head.

As he turned to go on, he spat speculatively. There was a sharp, explosive crackle that startled him. He spat again.

And again, in the air, before it could fall to the snow, the spittle crackled. He knew that at fifty below spittle crackled on the snow, but this spittle had crackled in the air. Undoubtedly it was colder than fifty below – how much colder he did not know. But the temperature did not matter. He was bound for the old claim on the left fork of Henderson Creek, where the boys were already. They had come over across the divide from the Indian Creek country, while he had come the roundabout way to take a look at the possibilities of getting out logs in the spring from the islands in the Yukon. He would be in to camp by six o'clock; a bit after dark, it was true, but the boys would be there, a fire would be going, and a hot supper would be ready. As for lunch, he pressed his hand against the protruding bundle under his jacket. It was also under his shirt, wrapped up in a handkerchief, and lying against the naked skin. It was the only way to keep the biscuits from freezing. He smiled agreeably to himself as he thought of those biscuits, each cut open and sopped in bacon grease, and each enclosing a generous slice of fried bacon.

He plunged in among the big spruce trees. The trail was faint. A foot of snow had fallen since the last sled had passed over, and he was glad he was without a sled, travelling light. In fact, he carried nothing but the lunch wrapped in the handkerchief. He was surprised, however, at the cold. It certainly was cold, he concluded, as he rubbed his numbed nose and cheek-bones with his mittened hand. He was a warm-whiskered man, but the hair on his face did not protect the high cheek-bones and the eager nose that thrust itself aggressively into the frosty air.

At the man's heels trotted a dog, a big native husky, the proper wolf-dog, grey-coated and without any visible or temperamental difference from its brother, the wild wolf. The animal was depressed by the tremendous cold. It knew that it was no time for travelling. Its instinct told it a truer tale than was told to the man by the man's judgment. In reality, it was not merely colder than fifty below zero; it was colder than sixty below, than seventy below. It was seventy-five below zero. Since the freezing-point is thirty-two above zero it meant that one hundred and seven degrees of frost obtained. The dog did not know anything about thermometers. Possibly in its brain there was no sharp consciousness of a condition of very cold such as was in the man's brain. But the brute had its instinct. It experienced a vague but menacing apprehension that subdued it and made it slink along at the man's heels, and that made it question eagerly every unwonted movement of the man as if expecting him to go into camp or to seek shelter somewhere and build a fire. The dog had learned fire, and it wanted fire, or else to burrow under the snow and cuddle its warmth away from the air.

The frozen moisture of its breathing had settled on its fur in a fine powder of frost, and especially were its jowls, muzzle, and eyelashes whitened by its crystalled breath. The man's red beard and moustache were like-wise frosted, but more solidly, the deposit taking the form of ice and increasing with every warm, moist breath he exhaled.

Also, the man was chewing tobacco, and the muzzle of ice held his lips so rigidly that he was unable to clear his chin when he expelled the juice. The result was that a crystal beard of the colour and solidity of amber was increasing its length on his chin. If he fell down it would shatter itself, like glass, into brittle fragments. But he did not mind the appendage. It was the penalty all tobacco-chewers paid in that country, and he had been out before in two cold snaps. They had not been so cold as this, he knew, but by the spirit thermometer at Sixty Mile he knew they had been registered at fifty below and at fifty-five.

He held on through the level stretch of woods for several miles, crossed a wide flat of nigger-heads, and dropped down a bank to the frozen bed of a small stream. This was Henderson Creek, and he knew he was ten miles from the forks. He looked at his watch. It was ten o'clock. He was making four miles an hour, and he calculated that he would arrive at the forks at half-past twelve. He decided to celebrate that event by eating his lunch there.

The dog dropped in again at his heels, with a tail drooping discouragement, as the man swung along the creek-bed. The furrow of the old sled-trail was plainly visible, but a dozen inches of snow covered the marks of the last runners, In a month no man had come up or down that silent creek. The man held steadily on. He was not much given to thinking, and just then particularly he had nothing to think about save that he would eat lunch at the forks and that at six o'clock he would be in camp with the boys. There was nobody to talk to; and, had there been, speech would have been impossible because of the ice-muzzle on his mouth. So he continued monotonously to chew tobacco and to increase the length of his amber beard.

Once in a while the thought reiterated itself that it was very cold and that he had never experienced such cold. As he walked along he rubbed his cheek-bones and nose with the back of his mittened hand. He did this automatically, now and again changing hands. But rub as he would, the instant he stopped his cheek-bones went numb, and the following instant the end of his nose went numb. He was sure to frost his cheeks; he knew that, and experienced a pang of regret that he had not devised a nose-strap of the sort Bud wore in cold snaps. Such a strap passed across the cheeks, as well, and saved them. But it didn't matter much, after all. What were frosted cheeks? A bit painful, that was all; they were never serious.

Empty as the man's mind was of thoughts, he was keenly observant, and he noticed the changes in the creek, the curves and bends and timber-jams, and always he sharply noted where he placed his feet. Once, coming around a bend, he shied abruptly, like a startled horse, curved away from the place where he had been walking, and retreated several paces back along the trail. The creek he knew was frozen clear to the bottom – no creek could contain water in that arctic winter – but he knew also that there were springs that bubbled out from the hillsides and ran along under the snow and on top the ice of the creek. He knew that the coldest snaps never froze these springs, and he knew likewise their danger. They were traps. They hid pools of water under the snow that might be three inches deep, or three feet. Sometimes a skin of ice half an inch thick covered them, and in turn was covered by the snow. Sometimes there were alternate layers of water and ice-skin, so that when one broke through he kept on breaking through for a while, sometimes wetting himself to the waist.

That was why he had shied in such panic. He had felt the ice give under his feet and heard the crackle of a snow-hidden ice-skin. And to get his feet wet in such a temperature meant trouble and danger. At the very least it meant delay, for he would be forced to stop and build a fire, and under its protection to bare his feet while he dried his socks and moccasins. He stood and studied the creek-bed and its banks, and decided that the flow of water came from the right. He reflected awhile, rubbing his nose and cheeks and skirted to the left, stepping gingerly and testing the footing for each step. Once clear of the danger, he took a fresh chew of tobacco and swung along at his four-mile gait.

In the course of the next two hours he came upon several similar traps. Usually the snow above the hidden pools had a sunken, candied appearance that advertised the danger. Once again, however, he had a close call; and once, suspecting danger, he compelled the dog to go on in front. The dog did not want to go. It hung back until the man shoved it forward, and then it went quickly across the white, unbroken surface. Suddenly it broke through, floundered to one side, and got away to firmer footing. It had wet its forefeet and legs and almost immediately the water that clung to it turned to ice. It made quick efforts to lick the ice off its legs, then dropped down in the snow and began to bite out the ice that had formed between the toes. This was a matter of instinct. To permit the ice to remain would mean sore feet. It did not know this. It merely obeyed the mysterious prompting that arose from the deep crypts of its being. But the man knew, having achieved a judgment on the subject, and he removed the mitten from his right hand and helped tear out the ice-particles. He did not expose his fingers more than a minute and was astonished at the swift numbness that smote them. It certainly was cold. He pulled on the mitten hastily, and beat the hand savagely across his chest.

At twelve o'clock the day was at its brightest. Yet the sun was too far south on its winter journey to clear the horizon. The bulge of the earth intervened between it and Henderson Creek, where the man walked under a clear sky at noon and cast no shadow. At half-past twelve, to the minute, he arrived at the forks of the creek. He was pleased at the speed he had made. If he kept it up, he would certainly be with the boys by six. He unbuttoned his jacket and shirt and drew forth his lunch. The action consumed no more than a quarter of a minute, yet in that brief moment the numbness laid hold of the exposed fingers. He did not put the mitten on, but, instead, struck the fingers a dozen sharp smashes against his leg. Then he sat down on a snow-covered log to eat. The sting that

76

followed upon the striking of his fingers against his leg ceased so quickly that he was startled. He had had no chance to take a bite of biscuit. He struck the fingers repeatedly and returned them to the mitten, baring the other hand for the purpose of eating. He tried to take a mouthful but the ice-muzzle prevented. He had forgotten to build a fire and thaw out. He chuckled at his foolishness, and as he chuckled he noted the numbness creeping into the exposed fingers. Also, he noted that the stinging which had first come to his toes when he sat down was already passing away. He wondered whether the toes were warm or numbed. He moved them inside the moccasins and decided that they were numbed.

He pulled the mitten on hurriedly and stood up. He was a bit frightened. He stamped up and down until the stinging returned into the feet. It certainly was cold was his thought. That man from Sulphur Creek had spoken the truth when telling how cold it sometimes got in the country. And he had laughed at him at the time! That showed one must not be too sure of things. There was no mistake about it, it was cold. He strode up and down, stamping his feet and threshing his arms, until reassured by the returning warmth. Then he got out matches and proceeded to make a fire. From the undergrowth, where high water of the previous spring had lodged a supply of seasoned twigs, he got his firewood. Working carefully from a small beginning, he soon had a roaring fire, over which he thawed the ice from his face and in the protection of which he ate his biscuits. For the moment the cold of space was outwitted. The dog took satisfaction in the fire, stretching out close enough for warmth and far enough away to escape being singed.

When the man had finished, he filled his pipe and took his comfortable time over a smoke. Then he pulled on his mittens, settled the ear-flaps of his cap firmly about his ears, and took the creek trail up the left fork. The dog was disappointed and yearned back towards the fire. This man did not know cold. Possibly all the generations of his ancestry had been ignorant of cold, of real cold, of cold one hundred and seven degrees below freezing-point. But the dog knew; all its ancestry knew, and it had inherited the knowledge. And it knew that it was not good to walk abroad in such fearful cold. It was the time to be snug in a hole in the snow and wait for a curtain of cloud to be drawn across the face of outer space whence this cold came. On the other hand, there was no keen intimacy between the dog and the man. The one was the toil-slave of the other, and the only caresses it had ever received were the caresses of the whiplash and of harsh and menacing throat-sounds that threatened the whip-lash. So the dog made no effort to communicate its apprehension to the man. It was not concerned in the welfare of the man; it was for its own sake that it yearned back towards the fire. But the man whistled, and spoke to it with the sound of whip-lashes, and the dog swung in at the man's heels and followed after.

The man took a chew of tobacco and proceeded to start a new amber beard. Also, his moist breath quickly powdered with white his moustache, eyebrows, and lashes. There did not seem to be so many springs on the left fork of the Henderson, and for half an hour the man saw no signs of any. And then it happened. At a place where there were no signs, where the soft, unbroken snow seemed to advertise solidity beneath, the man broke through. It was not deep. He wet himself halfway to the knees before he floundered out to the firm crust.

He was angry, and cursed his luck aloud. He had hoped to get into camp with the boys at six o'clock, and this would delay him an hour, for he would have to build a fire and dry out his footgear. This was imperative at that low temperature – he knew that much; and he turned aside to the bank, which he climbed. On top, tangled in the underbrush about the trunks of several small spruce trees, was a high-water deposit of dry fire-wood – sticks and twigs, principally, but also larger portions of seasoned branches and fine, dry, last-year's grasses. He threw down several large pieces on top of the snow. This served for a foundation and prevented the young flame from drowning itself in the snow it otherwise would melt. The flame he got by touching a match to a small shred of birch-bark that he took from his pocket. This burned even more readily than paper. Placing it on the foundation, he fed the young flames with wisps of dry grass and with the tiniest dry twigs.

He worked slowly and carefully, keenly aware of his danger. Gradually, as the flame grew stronger, he increased the size of the twigs with which he fed it. He squatted in the snow, pulling the twigs out from their entanglement in the brush and feeding directly to the flame. He knew there must be no failure. When it is seventy-five below zero, a man must not fail in his first attempt to build a fire – that is, if his feet are wet. If his feet are dry, and he fails, he can run along the trail for half a mile and restore his circulation. But the circulation of wet and freezing feet cannot be restored by running when it is seventy-five below. No matter how fast he runs, the wet feet will freeze the harder.

All this the man knew. The old-timer on Sulphur Creek had told him about it the previous fall, and now he was appreciating the advice. Already all sensation had gone out of his feet. To build the fire he had been forced to remove his mittens, and the fingers had quickly gone numb. His pace of four miles an hour had kept his heart pumping blood to the surface of his body and to all the extremities. But the instant he stopped, the action of the pump eased down. The cold of space smote the unprotected tip of the planet, and he, being on that unprotected tip, received the full force of the blow. The blood of his body recoiled before it. The blood was alive, like the dog, and like the dog it wanted to hide away and cover itself up from the fearful cold. So long as he walked four miles an hour, he pumped that blood, willy-nilly, to the surface; but now it ebbed away and sank down into the recesses of his body. The extremities were the first to feel its absence. His wet feet froze the faster, and his exposed fingers numbed the faster, though they had not yet begun to freeze. Nose and cheeks were already freezing, while the skin of all his body chilled as it lost its blood.

But he was safe. Toes and nose and cheeks would be only touched by the frost, for the fire was beginning to burn with strength. He was feeding it with twigs the size of his finger. In another minute he would be able to feed it with branches the size of his wrist, and then he could remove his wet footgear, and while it dried he could keep his naked feet warm by the fire, rubbing them at first, of course, with snow. The fire was a success. He was safe. He remembered the advice of the old-timer on Sulphur Creek, and smiled. The old-timer had been very serious in laying down the law that no man must travel alone in the Klondike after fifty below. Well, here he was; he had had an accident; he was alone; and he saved himself. Those old-timers were rather womanish, some of them, he thought. All a man had to do was to keep his head, and he was all right. Any man who was a man could travel alone. But it was surprising, the rapidity with which his cheeks and nose were freezing. And he had not thought his fingers could go lifeless in so short a time. Lifeless they were, for he could scarcely make them move together to grip a twig, and they seemed remote from his body and from him. When he touched a twig, he had to look and see whether or not he had hold of it. The wires were pretty well down between him and his finger-ends.

All of which counted for little. There was the fire, snapping and crackling and promising life with every dancing flame. He started to untie his moccasins. They were coated with ice; the thick German socks were like sheaths of iron halfway to the knees; and the moccasin strings were like rods of steel all twisted and knotted as by some conflagration. For a moment he tugged with his numbed fingers, then, realizing the folly of it, he drew his sheath-knife.

But before he could cut the strings, it happened. It was his own fault or, rather, his mistake. He should not have built the fire under the spruce tree. He should have built it in the open. But it had been easier to pull the twigs from the brush and drop them directly on the fire. Now the tree under which he had done this carried a weight of snow on its boughs. No wind had blown for weeks, and each bough was fully freighted. Each time he had pulled a twig he had communicated a slight agitation to the tree – an imperceptible agitation, so far as he was concerned, but an agitation sufficient to bring about the disaster. High up in the tree one bough capsized its load of snow. This fell on the boughs beneath, capsizing them. This process continued, spreading out and involving the whole tree. It grew like an avalanche, and it descended without warning upon the man and the fire, and the fire was blotted out! Where it had burned was a mantle of fresh and disordered snow.

The man was shocked. It was as though he had just heard his own sentence of death. For a moment he sat and stared at the spot where the fire had been. Then he grew very calm. Perhaps the old-timer on Sulphur Creek was right. If he had only had a trail-mate he would have been in no danger now. The trail-mate could have built the fire. Well, it was up to him to build the fire over again, and this second time there must be no failure. Even if he succeeded, he would most likely lose some toes. His feet must be badly frozen by now, and there would be some time before the second fire was ready.

Such were his thoughts, but he did not sit and think them. He was busy all the time they were passing through his mind. He made a new foundation for a fire, this time in the open, where no treacherous tree could blot it out. Next, he gathered dry grasses and tiny twigs from the high-water flotsam. He could not bring his fingers together to pull them out, but he was able to gather them by the handful. In this way he got many rotten twigs and bits of green moss that were undesirable, but it was the best he could do. He worked methodically, even collecting an armful of the larger branches to be used later when the fire gathered strength. And all the while the dog sat and watched him, a certain yearning wistfulness in its eyes, for it looked upon him as the fire-provider, and the fire was slow in coming.

When all was ready, the man reached in his pocket for a second piece of birch-bark. He knew the bark was there, and, though he could not feel it with his fingers, he could hear its crisp rustling as he fumbled for it. Try as he would, he could not clutch hold of it. And all the time, in his consciousness, was the knowledge that each instant his feet were freezing. This thought tended to put him in a panic, but he fought against it and kept calm. He pulled on his mittens with his teeth, and threshed his arms back and forth, beating his hands with all his might against his sides. He did this sitting down, and he stood up to do it; and all the while the dog sat in the snow, its wolf-brush of a tail curled around warmly over its forefeet, its sharp wolf-ears pricked forward intently as it watched the man. And the man as he beat and threshed with his arms and hands, felt a great surge of envy as he regarded the creature that was warm and secure in its natural covering.

After a time he was aware of the first far-away signals of sensation in his beaten fingers. The faint tingling grew stronger till it evolved into a stinging ache that was excruciating, but which the man hailed with satisfaction. He stripped the mitten from his right hand and fetched forth the birch-bark. The exposed fingers were quickly going numb again. Next he brought out his bunch of sulphur matches. But the tremendous cold had already driven the life out of his fingers. In his effort to separate one match from the others, the whole bunch fell in the snow. He tried to pick it out of the snow, but failed. The dead fingers could neither touch nor clutch. He was very careful. He drove the thought of his freezing feet, and nose, and cheeks, out of his mind, devoting his whole soul to the matches. He watched, using the sense of vision in place of that of touch, and when he saw his fingers on each side the bunch, he closed – that is, he willed to close them, for the wires were down, and the fingers did not obey. He pulled the mitten on the right hand, and beat it fiercely against his knee. Then, with both mittened hands, he scooped the bunch of matches, along with much snow, into his lap. Yet he was no better off.

After much manipulation he managed to get the bunch between the heels of his mittened hands. In this fashion he carried it to his mouth. The ice crackled and snapped when by a violent effort he opened his mouth. He drew the lower jaw in, curled the upper lip out of the way, and scraped the bunch with his upper teeth in order to separate a match. He succeeded in getting one, which he dropped on his lap. He was no better off. He could not pick it up. Then he devised a way. He picked it up in his teeth and scratched it on his leg. Twenty times he scratched before he succeeded in lighting it. As it flamed he held it with his teeth to the birch-bark. But the burning brimstone went up his nostrils and into his lungs, causing him to cough spasmodically. The match fell into the snow and went out.

The old-timer on Sulphur Creek was right, he thought in the moment of controlled despair that ensued: after fifty below, a man should travel with a partner. He beat his hands, but failed in exciting any sensation. Suddenly he bared both hands, removing the mittens with his teeth. He caught the whole bunch between the heels of his hands. His arm-muscles not being frozen enabled him to press the hand-heels tightly against the matches. Then he scratched the bunch along his leg. It flared into flame, seventy sulphur matches at once! There was no wind to blow them out. He kept his head to one side to escape the strangling fumes, and held the blazing bunch to the birch-bark. As he so held it, he became aware of sensation in his hand. His flesh was burning. He could smell it. Deep down below the surface he could feel it. The sensation developed into pain that grew acute. And still he endured it, holding the flame of the matches clumsily because his own burning hands were in the way, absorbing most of the flame.

At last, when he could endure no more, he jerked his hands apart. The blazing matches fell sizzling into the snow but the birch-bark was alight. He began laying dry grasses, and the tiniest twigs on the flame. He could not pick and choose, for he had to lift the fuel between the heels of his hands. Small pieces of rotten wood and green moss clung to the twigs, and he bit them off as well as he could with his teeth. He cherished the flame carefully and awkwardly. It meant life, and it must not perish. The withdrawal of blood from the surface of his body now made him begin to shiver, and he grew more awkward. A large piece of moss fell squarely on the little fire. He tried to poke it out with his fingers, but his shivering frame made him poke too far, and he disrupted the nucleus of the little fire, the burning grasses and tiny twigs separating and scattering. He tried to poke them together again, but in spite of the tenseness of the effort, his shivering got away with him, and the twigs were hopelessly scattered. Each twig gushed a puff of smoke and went out. The fire-provider had failed. As he looked apathetically about him, his eyes chanced on the dog, sitting across the ruins of the fire from him, in the snow, making restless, hunching movements, slightly lifting one forefoot and then the other, shifting its weight back and forth on them with wistful eagerness.

The sight of the dog put a wild idea into his head. He remembered the tale of the man, caught in a blizzard, who killed a steer and crawled inside the carcass, and so was saved. He would kill the dog and bury his hands in the warm body until the numbness went out of them. Then he could build another fire. He spoke to the dog, calling it to him; but in his voice was a strange note of fear that frightened the animal, who had never known the man to speak in such a way before. Something was the matter, and its suspicious nature sensed danger – it knew not what danger, but somewhere, somehow, in its brain arose an apprehension of the man. It flattened its ears down at the sound of the man's voice, and its restless, hunching movements and the liftings and shifting of its forefeet became more pronounced; but it would not come to the man. He got on his hands and knees and crawled towards the dog. This unusual posture again excited suspicion, and the animal sidled mincingly away.

The man sat up in the snow for a moment and struggled for calmness. Then he pulled on his mittens, by means of his teeth, and got upon his feet. He glanced down at first in order to assure himself that he was really standing up, for the absence of sensation in his feet left him unrelated to the earth. His erect position in itself started to drive the webs of suspicion from the dog's mind; and when he spoke peremptorily, with the sound of whip-lashes in his voice, the dog rendered its customary allegiance and came to him. As it came within reaching distance, the man lost his control. His arms flashed out to the dog and he experienced genuine surprise when he discovered that his hands could not clutch, that there was neither bend nor feeling in the fingers. He had forgotten for the moment that they were frozen and that they were freezing more and more. All this happened quickly, and before the animal could get away, he encircled its body with his arms. He sat down in the snow, and in this fashion held the dog, while it snarled and whined and struggled.

But it was all he could do, hold its body encircled in his arms and sit there. He realized that he could not kill the dog. There was no way to do it. With his helpless hands he could neither draw nor hold his sheath-knife nor throttle the animal. He released it, and it plunged wildly away, with tail between its legs, and still snarling. It halted forty feet away and surveyed him curiously, with ears sharply pricked forward. The man looked down at his hands in order to locate them, and found them hanging on the ends of his arms. It struck him as curious that one should have to use his eyes in order to find out where his hands were. He began threshing his arms back and forth, beating the mittened hands against his sides. He did this for five minutes, violently, and his heart pumped enough blood up to the surface to put a stop to his shivering. But no sensation was aroused in the hands. He had an impression that they hung like weights on the ends of his arms, but when he tried to run the impression down, he could not find it.

A certain fear of death, dull and oppressive, came to him. This fear quickly became poignant as he realized that it was no longer a mere matter of freezing his fingers and toes, or of his losing hands and feet, but that it was a matter of life and death with the chances against him. This threw him into a panic, and he turned and ran up the creek-bed along the old, dim trail. The dog joined in behind and kept up with him. He ran blindly, without intention, in fear such as he had never known in his life. Slowly, as he ploughed and floundered through the snow, he began to see things again – the banks of the creek, the old timber-jams, the leafless aspens, and the sky. The running made him feel better. He did not shiver. Maybe, if he ran on, his feet would thaw out; and, anyway, if he ran far enough, he would reach camp and the boys. Without doubt he would lose some fingers and toes and some of his face; but the boys would take care of him, and save the rest of him when he got there. And at the same time there was another thought in his mind that said he would never get to the camp and the boys; that it was too many miles away, that the freezing had too great a start on him, and that he would soon be stiff and dead. This thought he kept in the background and refused to consider. Sometimes it pushed itself forward and demanded to be heard, but he thrust it back and strove to think of other things.

It struck him as curious that he could run at all on feet so frozen that he could not feel them when they struck the earth and took the weight of his body. He seemed to himself to skim along above the surface and to have no connection with the earth. Somewhere he had once seen a winged Mercury, and he wondered if Mercury felt as he felt when skimming over the earth.

His theory of running until he reached camp and the boys had one flaw in it; he lacked the endurance. Several times he stumbled, and finally he tottered, crumpled up, and fell. When he tried to rise, he failed. He must sit and rest, he decided, and next time he would merely walk and keep on going. As he sat and regained his breath, he noted that he was feeling quite warm and comfortable. He was not shivering, and it even seemed that a warm glow had come to his chest and trunk. And yet, when he touched his nose or cheeks, there was no sensation. Running would not thaw them out. Nor would it thaw out his hands and feet. Then the thought came to him that the frozen portions of his body must be extending. He tried to keep this thought down, to forget it, to think of something else; he was aware of the panicky feeling that it caused, and he was afraid of the panic. But the thought asserted itself, and persisted, until it produced a vision of his body totally frozen. This was too much, and he made another wild run along the trail. Once he slowed down to a walk, but the thought of the freezing extending itself made him run again.

And all the time the dog ran with him, at his heels. When he fell down a second time, it curled its tail over its forefeet and sat in front of him, facing him, curiously eager and intent. The warmth and security of the animal angered him, and he cursed it till it flattened down its ears appeasingly. This time the shivering came more quickly upon the man. He was losing in his battle with the frost. It was creeping into his body from all sides. The thought of it drove him on, but he ran no more than a hundred feet, when he staggered and pitched headlong. It was his last panic. When he had recovered his breath and control, he sat up and entertained in his mind the conception of meeting death with dignity. However, the conception did not come to him in such terms. His idea of it was that he had been making a fool of himself, running around like a chicken with its head cut off – such was the simile that occurred to him. Well, he was bound to freeze anyway, and he might as well take it decently. With this new-found peace of mind came the first glimmerings of drowsiness. A good idea, he thought, to sleep off to death. It was like taking an anaesthetic. Freezing was not so bad as people thought. There were lots worse ways to die.

He pictured the boys finding his body next day. Suddenly he found himself with them, coming along the trail and looking for himself. And, still with them, he came around a turn in the trail and found himself lying in the snow. He did not belong with himself any more, for even then he was out of himself, standing with the boys and looking at himself in the snow. It certainly was cold was his thought. When he got back to the States he could tell the folks what real cold was. He drifted on from this to a vision of the old-timer on Sulphur Creek. He could see him quite clearly, warm and comfortable, and smoking a pipe.

'You were right, old hoss; you were right,' the man mumbled to the old-timer of Sulphur Creek.

Then the man drowsed off into what seemed to him the most comfortable and satisfying sleep he had ever known. The dog sat facing him and waiting. The brief day drew to a close in a long, slow twilight. There were no signs of a fire to be made, and, besides, never in the dog's experience had it known a man to sit like that in the snow and make no fire. As the twilight drew on, its eager yearning for the fire mastered it, and with a great lifting and shifting of forefeet, it whined softly, then flattened its ears down in anticipation of being chidden by the man. But the man remained silent. Later, the dog whined loudly. And still later it crept close to the man and caught the scent of death. This made the animal bristle and back away. A little longer it delayed, howling under the stars that leaped and danced and shone brightly in the cold sky. Then it turned and trotted up the trail in the direction of the camp it knew, where were the other food-providers and fire-providers.

Marriage of the Dead

Li Rui

In front of the courtyard gate, a worn spindle of jujube wood twirled swiftly in hoary hands, one strand of creamy linen after another wound on to it seemingly without end, together with wisps of time. The afternoon sunlight, crumbled by the vast yellow land, spread itself kindly. One suddenly felt that the setting sun was declining not into the mountains in the west but into the old woman's weak eyes.

Not far away, several men were digging up the grave under her husband's direction. Spades and picks kept hitting bricks and stones and chill, metallic clanks crumbled into the gentleness of sunset. He had been Party secretary of the village, and although that had been quite some time ago, the grave had remained a weight on his mind.

It had stood there alone for all of fourteen years, and the young Beijing woman in it had herself long turned to yellow soil.

'If the poor girl hadn't died, she'd have been up to her knees in kids by now.'

A strand of woman's sympathy for women was spun into the hempen yarn tight around the spindle: it was a happy day for the young woman, for today she would be reburied with her man. The villagers had temporised and discussed, discussed and temporised, and in the end got the money to buy a 'man' as helpmate for her who had been alone in her grave for fourteen years. A fortune-teller had been hired and concluded that the horoscopes tallied.

Beside the grave rested two brightly-painted coffins, intended for skeletons and so not big, each with a red ribbon tied to it. The bones of the purchased dead man had been laid in one of the decorated caskets; the other was empty. When the men had opened the grave and taken her from her resting place of fourteen years, they would place her in it and bury them together, after which one person from every family was to go to the cave of the village head for buckwheat, noodles with boiled mutton and carrots in thick gravy. Her loneliness made their hearts ache, with her parents far, far away in Beijing, her classmates gone without looking back and only she left here. She had passed through the land of the living all alone, so her marriage in the underworld should be celebrated elaborately and extravagantly.

As the spades and picks came up against the brick-and-mortar grave mound, the odd spark shot into the dry air. Someone brought up the worrying subject of the harvest.

'If it doesn't rain now, we'll have a drought on our hands come autumn …'

A drought and its repercussions were as clear as could be, so no-one responded over the random clanging.

'With a downpour like that year's we'd have nothing to worry about.'

A man paused: 'If it hadn't been so heavy, Yuxiang wouldn't have died'.

They all stopped, old memories surfacing in their minds.

'Do you think it was the black snake sent the rain that year?'

'Superstition again!' said the ex-secretary with a frown.

'I don't mean to be superstitious, but the black serpent's quite an omen.'

'It's superstition!' repeated the ex-secretary with a second frown.

The other was not convinced: 'Then what's wrong with the kids in the school? Loads of them fall ill. Even the teacher's come down with it. I never wanted Yuxiang's memorial hall used as a school. There's no worse luck than a lonely ghost.'

'Suppose we don't use the memorial hall; is anyone going to build a village school?'

'We would have had a school if we had made less of those terraced fields ... And Yuxiang probably wouldn't have been killed if she hadn't gone with you to make them!'

The retort was too cutting.

The ex-secretary was momentarily at a loss. As he pulled the burning cigarette from his mouth, a shimmering thread of saliva that extended from its butt was torn apart. Suddenly he burst into a fit of coughing which reddened his face. Long ago though it had been, the fact that he had been Party secretary was not a thing either the villagers or he himself could have forgotten.

Someone tried to smooth things over. 'You can't say that. It's all a matter of fate whether you live or die.

Nobody has any control over anybody. Without the black snake, Yuxiang would have been alive today. The black snake's a monster all right; it just crept up when the rope was tossed out ...'

The topic had been gone over again and again for fourteen years, and no-one around had the slightest interest in doing so yet again. The cold, metallic clangs started up again.

It had been a year when all the villagers and the high school graduates from Beijing worked hard under the Party secretary for a winter and a spring, and raised three tidy, level terraced fields, for which they had won a red flag, though the first mountain torrents of summer had washed away two of the fields. At the second flood, the young graduates had taken the red flag from the home of the Party secretary to the field, stuck it at the edge, and pledged to fight the flood and save the field. Like a raging bull, the waters had engulfed the field dam in the blink of an eye. The young graduates had jumped in hand in hand, like they did in the films. The old Party secretary had knelt down on the ground in the rain and kowtowed till his forehead bled, begging them to come out. By the time the others had been pulled from the water, the collapsing dam had dragged Yuxiang into the current. Men ran after her for several dozen metres with a rope. Now and then she appeared above the surface flailing her arms and had at last caught the rope that was tossed to her. But as the men pooled their strength to haul it in, all at once they had seen a thick black snake with its rear section coiled tightly round her waist as it crawled up the rope at lightning speed, its long forked tongue darting right and left from its upraised head. Its dripping body had shimmered coldly, and in a blink of the eye, it had advanced three or four metres. The rope crew had shrieked and all let go, and the long, thick rope together with the snake had splashed into the water and disappeared beneath the waves. Only at the bend fifteen kilometres downstream had her corpse been washed on to the bank. The searchers had said the waters could strip the clothes off you, and Yuxiang had not a stitch on her: a tender, white body such as they had never seen had been ringed at the waist by a livid bruise where the snake had wrapped itself around her.

Then she had got into the newspaper. Then the Party secretary of the county had held a thousand-strong rally. Then the memorial hall block had been built. Then there had been the grave and the stone in front of it, reading:

AN EXAMPLE TO SCHOOL-LEAVERS, A HEROINE
OF THE LULIANG MOUNTAINS.

With, on the back:

CHENG YUXIANG, BORN IN A RAILWAY WORKER'S
FAMILY IN BEIJING MAY 5,1953;
GRADUATED FROM BEIJING NO. 37
MIDDLE SCHOOL 1968. SETTLED IN
SHENYU VILLAGE, TUYAO BRIGADE,
CHASHANG COMMUNE, LULIANG MOUNTAIN
REGION, JANUARY 1969.

HEROICALLY GAVE HER LIFE FIGHTING
FLOODS TO SAVE TERRACED FIELDS
AUGUST 17,1972.

After this there had been no more news reports or meetings, but the thought of her lonely grave at the end of the village had disturbed the villagers:

'Shouldn't think the place could be clean with a lonely ghost left at the south end of the village.'

But for fear of hurting the feelings of her classmates, and, more importantly, of flouting the decision of the County Party Committee, the grave still stood at the end of the village. Neither the newspaper nor the inscription had mentioned the black snake, but the villagers could not forget the daunting scene and always firmly believed that some sadness, however hard to put a finger on, gathered in the bricks and mortar of that grave. Fourteen years had slipped by. Her classmates had gone and would not be back; a number of people had filled the office of Party secretary of the county; none remembered the young woman as the green grass grew slowly out of the chinks in the brickwork.

After the brickwork had been removed, the spades worked much more freely in the soft yellow earth. Gradually the men sank into the pit, until only the silver tips of the spades hurling yellow wetness out of the pit glistened in the sun. A foot trod on nothing, and a spade fell deep into empty space. Expected though this was, the men's hearts still leapt.

'Reached it?'

'Yes.'

'Steady on. Don't damage her.'

'I know.'

The ex-secretary handed down the waiting liquor bottle.

'A mouthful, all of you, against the damp down there.'

All the men, drinkers or not, took a gulp. The strong smell of liquor wafted from the grave pit.

Made of bad wood, the coffin had rotted, and when the decayed lid was removed by hand, the complete skeleton shone whitely. The atmosphere in the pit once again froze with tension. This, too, was expected, but all were rooted to the spot with terror before the bones all the same. All those who had seen the delicate pale flesh that had clothed the skeleton fourteen years before still remembered the talking, laughing woman it had supported. When the torrent had swallowed her up, her long pigtails had floated back to the surface of the water, and the red wool binding them had flashed back into view; yet now a gleaming skeleton lay in the yellow earth, and a still distinguishable smell of decay rose from the mud and bones at the bottom of the grave.

The ex-secretary passed down the new coffin. 'Quick, shift Yuxiang into this, head first.'

They squatted down anyhow, and the hollow thump of bones on wood took over for a while. The bones and the sound led to an age-old yet peaceful topic.

'It all comes down to the same thing, for emperors and all.'

'You can go at any age, but what gets me is, if she was going to die, why did she have to come all the way from Beijing to do it?'

'Won't the yellow earth there take burials?'

'Nothing like here. I bet they don't have such big memorial meetings when you die.'

'I won't need one, just a son to carry my flag of mourning and a band to play.'

'That's feudal,' said the ex-secretary, turning serious.

'Oh no, you aren't feudal,' mocked someone. 'When you die, you'll get burned up like a good civil servant, bit by bit over a slow flame. I'll drive you off in a cart when the time comes.'

Laughter burst from the grave pit and was cut off abruptly as the ex-secretary coughed himself crimson in the face, while two tears spilled from his blood-red eye sockets. Suddenly there was a shout.

'Oh, look! That thing's still there!'

Four or five heads bunched together and a dozen eyes opened wide around a red plastic cover.

'It was Yuxiang's!'

'It's the *Quotations from Chairman Mao* she always used.'

'Ah ...'

'Oh ...'

The mood within the walls of the grave wavered uncertainly between surprise, praise and fear. It was actually blood-curdling to have the past dug up alive like that.

'What shall we do with it?' asked someone hesitantly. 'Move it for her?'

The ex-secretary erupted.

'Why not?' he bawled at the men down in the pit. 'You prefer to keep it yourself and make your bloody fortune? Move it! Every hair belongs to her. Move!'

The men were browbeaten into a cowed silence. The sound of their heavy panting rang out alone and loudly.

The quarrel must have been heard, for the spindle at the courtyard gate stopped and a hoary hand was raised to shade a brow.

'Is today the day to throw your weight about, you old dotard?'

The dug grave was closed again, except for the original cover of brickwork. The new mound of yellow earth stood out plainly and looked peaceful and calm in the vast yellow land, and the kindly setting sun seemed as if it was truly appeased at last.

The ex-secretary tore open the last packet of cigarettes bought in the village and counted. Just enough for two more each. After he had passed them out, he shook the bottle and found there was still something at the bottom, so the lot of them sat on the ground before the grave and took a drink while they smoked. One round warmed everyone's spirits.

'What shall we do with the stone?' asked one, poking a cigarette at the grave.

'With what?'

'The stone. There was only Yuxiang buried there before, and the stone was just for her. But now there are two of them, and he has a name too. If it comes to that, he's the head of the family!'

It was a problem.

They brooded, puffs of smoke emerging above their heads. Through its veil, one person was looking at the ex-secretary. The old man swallowed a mouthful of liquor, the heat of which burned all the way down to the bottom of his heart.

'No need. Let him put up with it. Yuxiang earned that stone with her life. Never mind about anybody else. People in this village have to remember that!'

No one made a reply. More puffs of smoke emerged. The ex-secretary stood up and slapped the dust off his behind.

'Back for buckwheat noodles!'

At the sight of them dispersing from the grave, the twirling spindle stopped once more. She pulled off a strand of linen and put it into her mouth. As she slowly smoothed it with her saliva, she pondered over the task entrusted to her by her husband. While the sinking of the late sun expanded the desolate mountain country, placid thoughts were drawn slowly from the thread in her mouth and melted in the thickening dusk.

After their noodles, the old couple sat by the twirling spindle, till at midnight it stopped.

'Shall I go now?'

'Yes.'

She handed him a basket that she had prepared.

'Everything's there, cigarettes, liquor, food and incense. Have a look.'

'That's fine.'

'Tell Yuxiang when you go that the lad was born in the Year of the Snake – couldn't be a better match. In the land of the living we marry flesh and blood. In the underworld they do better and marry bones. Bones make a proper marriage!'

'More superstition!'

'If you aren't superstitious, why did you wait till midnight?'

'That's different!'

'How? Anyway I know she was a wretched girl. She lived in our cave for two years. She's as good as my own daughter. . .'

Her tears came faster than her words. Exasperated with them, he turned and went. It was very dark, with neither stars nor moon.

The russet spindle twirled again under the oil lamp, evenly taking strand after strand of linen. All at once a violent fit of coughing came from the graveside; she turned her head anxiously. The cough leapt from the dank depths of the black night as if from the hollow decayed bole of an old tree, resembling both weeping and laughter.

Others were awakened in the caves of the village, their rigid forms buried deep in the darkness, their ears pricked up in apprehension.

Translated by Wu Jingchao

A Gentleman's Agreement

Elizabeth Jolley

In the home-science lesson I had to unpick my darts as
Mrs Kay said they were all wrong and then I scorched the
collar of my dress because I had the iron too hot. And then
the sewing-machine needle broke and there wasn't a spare
and Mrs Kay got really wild and Peril Page cut all the
notches off her pattern by mistake and that finished
everything.

'I'm not ever going back to that school,' I said to Mother
in the evening. 'I'm finished with that place!' So that was
my brother and me both leaving school before we should
have and my brother kept leaving jobs too, one job after
another, sometimes not even staying long enough in one
place to wait for his pay.

But Mother was worrying about what to get for my
brother's tea.

'What about a bit of lamb's fry and bacon,' I said. She
brightened up then and, as she was leaving to go up the
terrace for her shopping, she said, 'You can come with me
tomorrow then and we'll get through the work quicker.'
She didn't seem to mind at all that I had left school.

Mother cleaned in a large block of luxury apartments.
She had keys to the flats and she came and went as she
pleased and as her work demanded. It was while she was
working there that she had the idea of letting the people
from down our street taste the pleasures rich people took

for granted in their way of living. While these people were away to their offices or on business trips she let our poor neighbours in. We had wedding receptions and parties in the penthouse and the old folk came in to soak their feet and wash their clothes while Mother was doing the cleaning. As she said, she gave a lot of pleasure to people without doing anybody any harm though it was often a terrible rush for her. She could never refuse anybody anything and, because of this, always had more work than she could manage and more people to be kind to than her time really allowed.

Sometimes at the weekends I went with Mother to look at Grandpa's valley. It was quite a long bus ride. We had to get off at the twenty-nine-mile peg, cross the Medulla Brook, and walk up a country road with scrub on either side till we came to some cleared acres of pasture which was the beginning of her father's land. She struggled through the wire fence, hating the mud. She wept out loud because the old man hung on to his land and all his money was buried, as she put it, in the sodden meadows of capeweed and stuck fast in the outcrops of granite higher up where all the topsoil had washed away. She couldn't sell the land because Grandpa was still alive in a home for the aged, and he wanted to keep the farm though he couldn't do anything with it. Even sheep died there. They either starved or got drowned, depending on the time of the year. It was either drought there or flood.

The weatherboard house was so neglected it was falling apart, the tenants were feckless, and if a calf was born there it couldn't get up. That was the kind of place it was. When we went to see Grandpa he wanted to know about the farm and Mother tried to think of things to please him. She didn't say the fence posts were crumbling away and that the castor-oil plants had taken over the yard so you couldn't get through to the barn.

There was an old apricot tree in the middle of the meadow, it was as big as a house and a terrible burden to us to get the fruit at just the right time. Mother liked to take some to the hospital so that Grandpa could keep up his pride and self-respect a bit.

In the full heat of the day I had to pick with an apron tied around me. It had deep pockets for the fruit. I grabbed at the green fruit when I thought Mother wasn't looking and pulled off whole branches so it wouldn't be there to be picked later.

'Don't take that branch!' Mother screamed from the ground 'Them's not ready yet. We'll have to come back tomorrow for them.'

I lost my temper and pulled off the apron full of fruit and hurled it down but it stuck on a branch and hung there, quite out of reach either from up the tree where I was or from the ground.

'Wait! Just you wait till I get a holt of you!' Mother pranced round the tree and I didn't come down till we had missed our bus and it was getting dark and all the dogs in the little township barked as if they were insane, the way dogs do in the country, as we walked through trying to get a lift home.

One Sunday in the winter it was very cold but Mother thought we should go all the same. We passed some sheep huddled in a natural fold of furze and withered grass all frost sparkling in the morning.

'Quick!' Mother said. 'We'll grab a sheep and take a bit of wool back to Grandpa.'

'But they're not our sheep,' I said.

'Never mind!' And she was in among the sheep before I could stop her. The noise was terrible but she managed to grab a bit of wool.

'It's terrible dirty and shabby,' she complained, pulling at the shreds with her cold fingers. 'I don't think I've ever seen such miserable wool.'

All that evening she was busy with the wool, she did make me laugh.

'How will modom have her hair done?' She put the wool on the kitchen table and kept walking all round it talking to it. She tried to wash it and comb it but it still looked awful so she put it round one of my curlers for the night.

'I'm really ashamed of the wool,' Mother said next morning.

'But it isn't ours,' I said.

'I know but I'm ashamed all the same,' she said. So when we were in the penthouse at South Heights she cut a tiny piece off the bathroom mat. It was so soft and silky. And later we went to visit Grandpa. He was sitting with his poor paralysed legs under his tartan rug.

'Here's a bit of the wool clip, Dad,' Mother said, bending over to kiss him. His whole face lit up.

'That's nice of you to bring it, really nice.' His old fingers stroked the little piece of nylon carpet. 'It's very good, deep and soft.' He smiled at Mother.

'They do wonderful things with sheep these days, Dad,' she said.

'They do indeed,' he said, and all the time he was feeling the bit of carpet.

'Are you pleased, Dad?' Mother asked him anxiously. 'You are pleased, aren't you?'

'Oh yes, I am,' he assured her.

I thought I saw a moment of disappointment in his eyes, but the eyes of old people often look full of tears.

On the way home I tripped on the steps.

'Ugh! I felt your bones!' Really Mother was so thin it hurt to fall against her.

'Well, what d'you expect me to be, a boneless wonder?'

Really Mother had such a hard life and we lived in such a cramped and squalid place. She longed for better things and she needed a good rest. I wished more than anything the old man would agree to selling his land. Because he wouldn't sell, I found myself wishing he would die and whoever really wants to wish someone to die! It was only that it would sort things out a bit for us.

In the supermarket Mother thought and thought what she could get for my brother for his tea. In the end all she could come up with was fish fingers and a packet of jelly beans.

'You know I never eat fish! And I haven't eaten sweets in years.' My brother looked so tall in the kitchen. He lit a cigarette and slammed out and Mother was too tired and too upset to eat her own tea.

Grandpa was an old man and though his death was expected, it was unexpected really and it was a shock to Mother to find she suddenly had eighty-seven acres to sell. And there was the house too. She had a terrible lot to do as she decided to sell the property herself and, at the same time, she did not want to let down the people at South Heights. There was a man interested to buy the land. Mother had kept him up her sleeve for years, ever since he had stopped once by the bottom paddock to ask if it was for sale. At the time Mother would have given her right arm to be able to sell it and she promised he should have first refusal if it ever came on the market.

We all three, Mother and myself and my brother went out at the weekend to tidy things up. We lost my brother and then we suddenly saw him running and running and shouting, his voice lifting up in the wind as he raced up the slope of the valley.

'I do believe he's laughing! He's happy!' Mother just stared at him and she looked so happy too.

I don't think I ever saw the country look so lovely before.

The tenant was standing by the shed. The big tractor had crawled to the doorway like a sick animal and had stopped there, but in no time my brother had it going.

It seemed there was nothing my brother couldn't do. Suddenly after doing nothing in his life he was driving the tractor and making fire breaks, he started to paint the sheds and he told Mother what fencing posts and wire to order. All these things had to be done before the sale could go through. We all had a wonderful time in the country. I kept wishing we could live in the house. All at once it seemed lovely there at the top of the sunlit meadow. But I knew that however many acres you have they aren't any use unless you have money too. I think we were all thinking this but no one said anything though Mother kept looking at my brother and the change in him.

There was no problem about the price of the land. This man, he was a doctor, really wanted it and Mother really needed the money.

'You might as well come with me,' Mother said to me on the day of the sale. 'You can learn how business is done.' So we sat in this lawyer's comfortable room and he read out from various papers and the doctor signed things and Mother signed. Suddenly she said to them, 'You know my father really loved his farm but he only managed to have it late in life and then he was never able to live there because of his illness.' The two men looked at her.

'I'm sure you will understand,' she said to the doctor, 'with your own great love of the land, my father's love for his valley. I feel if I could live there just to plant one crop and stay while it matures, my father would rest easier in his grave.'

Well, I don't see why not.' The doctor was really a kind man. The lawyer began to protest, he seemed quite angry.

'It's not in the agreement,' he began to say. But the doctor silenced him, he got up and came round to Mother's side of the table.

'I think you should live there and plant your one crop and stay while it matures,' he said to her. 'It's a gentleman's agreement,' he said.

'That's the best sort.' Mother smiled up at him and they shook hands.

'I wish your crop well,' the doctor said, still shaking her hand.

The doctor made the lawyer write out a special clause which they all signed. And then we left, everyone satisfied.

Mother had never had so much money and the doctor had the valley at last, but it was the gentleman's agreement which was the best part.

My brother was impatient to get on with improvements.

'There's no rush,' Mother said.

'Well, one crop isn't very long,' he said.

'It's long enough.' she said.

So we moved out to the valley and the little weather-board cottage seemed to come to life very quickly with the pretty things we chose for the rooms.

'It's nice whichever way you look out from these little windows,' Mother was saying and just then her crop arrived. The carter set down the boxes along the edge of the veranda and, when he had gone, my brother began to unfasten the hessian coverings. Inside were hundreds of seedlings in little plastic containers.

'What are they?' he asked.

'Our crop,' Mother said.

'Yes, I know, but what is the crop? What are these?'

'Them,' said Mother. She seemed unconcerned. 'Oh they're a jarrah forest,' she said.

'But that will take years and years to mature,' he said.

'I know,' Mother said. 'We'll start planting tomorrow. We'll pick the best places and clear and plant as we go along.'

'But what about the doctor?' I said. Somehow I could picture him, pale and patient by his car out on the lonely road which went through his valley. I seemed to see him looking with longing at his paddocks and his meadows and at his slopes of scrub and bush.

'Well, he can come on his land whenever he wants to have a look at us,' Mother said. 'There's nothing in the gentleman's agreement to say he can't.'

Private Eloy

Samuel Feijoo

Eloy was born in the valley of Vega Vieja of peasant parents: his mother a hardworking, smiling mulatto woman, his father a hefty Galician who boasted that he had laid more rails in the region of San Juan de Potrerillo than any man on earth. Eloy was the fifth child in a family of nine.

From the time he was very small Eloy knew the land. He was obliged to work hard, from milking-time in the chill of 2am, when he had to take care of the calves, to the hoeing, the ploughing, the selling of the milk in the far-off town. There was not much schooling for Eloy. His mother barely taught him his first letters. His father, an illiterate who could not resign himself to his ignorance, lamented the lack of a school in the valley. Often he would say to his wife, 'If the children could only study a little they could get away from this slavery in the fields. Here they'll throw their lives away working and end up with nothing.'

But no teacher came to the valley of Vega Vieja. Who did come were the Rural Police, the pair of them, riding fat horses, receiving greetings and offerings – a turkey, a couple of chickens – from the intimidated peasants watching the police with ancestral fear. And the peddler of clothes and trinkets, he came, and so did the politician full of smiles and back-slapping, looking for votes and promising projects that never came to anything.

115

And it was one of these well-dressed, two-faced politicians who, years later, noticed that under his rags Eloy had the same robust body as his father and proposed to the family, 'If you get me a hundred votes in the Vega Vieja district I'll get him into the army for you … But fair's fair. You bring me a hundred pledged votes and I'll fix it with the Colonel.'

This promise fell on Eloy's ears like spring rain on thirsty maize fields. It was irresistible. Although the family had some doubts at first, knowing the politician's lying tongue, they finally came to a decision. 'If he gets into the army the boy's made. Not much work and a pay-packet. Free clothes and food and some money to help us out a bit …'

But the prudent Galician was not happy about it. 'If you're a soldier you're the lowest card in the pack. You get kicked around by everyone from the corporal to the lieutenant. He won't study at all, he'll just take orders, no education, nothing and he'll probably end up behaving like all the rest …'

But nobody took any notice of him. The family rushed out to look for votes and got promises from half Vega Vieja and even further afield. The result was astounding: more than a hundred pledges. The politician was informed, he collected the list and a few days later he was back with Eloy's papers.

He embraced the young *guajiro*, handed him an envelope and said, 'Fair's fair. Here's your posting. Take this envelope and report to the headquarters in Las Villas.'

And with more embraces all round he went off very pleased with himself, taking the new soldier with him. Eloy was carrying a little bundle containing a change of linen underwear, a pair of socks, a shirt and a spare pair of trousers. He was wearing a *guayabera* of coarse drill, his Sunday best, and thick trousers bagging heavily at the knees in spite of the shiny starch.

At headquarters he was assigned to Santa Clara barracks. There he made friends among the soldiers, peasants like himself, and adapted easily to the discipline of the job. And he felt happy, proud of his khaki uniform and of the arms he carried which gave him a new authority. He had a sense of his importance and enjoyed his position which had rescued him from poverty and toil with no future but a miserable hut and a thankless struggle with the soil.

To begin with he helped his parents with a few pesos and went to visit them in his new uniform, dazzling his family and the neighbours with his rifle and his soldier's trappings, his shiny boots and his complexion, already so much lighter. Eloy was happy.

But his prudent Galician father asked, 'Are you studying?' 'Not yet,' answered his son. 'That's bad. You'll be nothing but a turnip with a tie on. Well-dressed and clean outside and an ignorant clodhopper inside.'

They laughed and said goodbye. And Eloy went back to the city barracks and carried on just the same, without studying, as he couldn't be bothered with reading, and anyway his life was easy. He knew the value of a peso so he did not waste his money. And he went on helping his parents until he met Eulalia.

His small wages went on her, in presents and taking her out. And one night he carried her off. He rented a room, furnished it sparsely and then Eloy began to feel the pinch. He loved Eulalia and took care that she didn't want for anything.

One afternoon as he was leaving the barracks Lieutenant Valladares said to him, 'You can't go home. We've got an eviction tomorrow in Rio Chiquito.'

Eloy didn't understand what it was all about, but as usual he obeyed. That was the first thing he had been taught, blind obedience to his superiors. He sent a message to Eulalia and resigned himself to the situation.

At dawn they rode out into the countryside. Surrounded by the wildness of nature, the lonely woodland and savannah, with the morning sun shining, the birds singing, the vultures wheeling, the scent of lianas and tender leaves, Eloy felt the joy of his childhood, he was back in his own element. The sun in the open country was doing him good. He rode along cheerfully. He hummed a song.

After six hours' riding they reached Rio Chiquito. There he saw them, at the door of the hut. Their torn clothes, their thin, dry faces, their bare feet, the half-naked children in their arms. Their lifeless eyes. Their silent, pale lips.

The Lieutenant said to them, 'You've got to leave. You're being evicted ...'

The head of the family replied humbly, 'We don't know where to go.' The Lieutenant answered, 'We're sorry, we really are sorry. But the law's the law. You've got to get out.' An old man said, 'The law is unjust. We always pay the rent.' The Lieutenant replied, 'I've got the legal warrant here – and that's what counts. The land isn't yours and you've got to go. Start loading your stuff onto the cart because we're here to see that the law is carried out.'

Eloy watched the eviction, in silence, disturbed. He saw the thin arms straining to heave the shabby iron beds onto the cart, the wardrobe with two planks missing at the back, the pine table half eaten away by termites, three stools, a cradle with the paint peeling, bundles of clothes, a wooden plough, the stone water-filter, the wash-basin ... and he thought of his family, thought that the same thing might happen to them.

And Eloy was troubled.

They escorted the evicted family to a boundary of coconut palms and after watching them disappear down a lane they went back to the hut and burnt as the Lieutenant ordered.

Eloy, holding a flaming branch, his face glowing in the firelight, felt uneasy.

On the way back, as his horse trotted along briskly, nature did not seem so beautiful any more. He felt guilty. He thought of the evicted peasants, of what their fate would be in that countryside where work was non-existent. Facing the rigours of the 'dead season' ...

When he reached the barracks he felt ill. And that night he found no happiness in Eulalia's arms.

His other disagreeable mission happened during the sugar harvest. There was a strike of workers who were not being paid a fair wage. His detachment arrived in the forecourt of the paralysed refinery. Eloy, together with other soldiers, arrested some workers. He took them out of their houses and made them get into lorries to be taken to the city prisons. He saw them close up, some were peasants like himself. They were justifying themselves, 'We're on strike because they won't give us our rights.' 'Get into the lorry. I don't want any lip from you,' said the lieutenant.

None of the workers put up any resistance against the weapons pointing at them. They climbed into the lorry with an expression of determination. Eloy watched them leave, a twinge of anguish in his heart.

That same day he patrolled the canefields. Rifle in hand, he walked round the boundaries ready to fire at any striker who might try to set fire to the sugar-cane.

The next day, as he was standing sentinel in the deserted forecourt, a little boy came up to him. 'Guard, mama is ill and needs to go to the doctor. Help me to lift her up. There's no one here. They've all gone.'

Eloy went into the hut and lifted an emaciated woman from the floor. 'She has attacks,' said the child. 'And your father?' asked Eloy. 'He's in prison.' Eloy looked at him uneasily. The unconscious woman sighed faintly. She stretched her limbs and opened her eyes. Eloy quickly asked her. 'Your husband, where is he?' 'He is a striker. He's in prison,' murmured the woman.

Eloy looked at the hut and saw the poverty, the same that he knew so well, the same as in his own hut. He saw the shabby stove with its clay pot, the broken-seated chairs, the beds covered with rags. 'He's in prison,' repeated the little boy.

Eloy was getting fat. He found the life easy. He asked for nothing more. His was a life of simple routine, very different from the heavy labour in the fields where he had had no clean clothes, no good shoes, no money. He would not have changed his status as a soldier for anything in the world. He knew poverty and its despair at close quarters. Nobody was going to make him give up his uniform and his salary. Not even his Eulalia. Nor his two-year-old son. It was a life without ups and downs. Get paid, follow the routine and live … No other ideas bothered him much. Politics or injustices or crimes. He was safe. That was how the world was and he had a position in the world, that of a soldier. And that was enough for him. But every now and then he didn't forget the evicted family and the striker's little boy.

In the world around him, not everything was going well for the government. There had been risings in the mountains against the crimes. Despotism was reaping its natural harvest and now the soldiers were going out to fight the rebels in the mountains. The days were not peaceful any more. The war was a bitter reality which he had to face up to. Eloy was not a coward. Eloy knew how to obey. Eloy went to the front.

Eulalia hung religious medals round his neck. She made him accept a charm to ward off bullets, embroidered by her with the Sacred Heart of Jesus in red to protect him from death. She gave him the Prayer of the Just Judge for him to read and carry with him. And Eloy accepted it with a smile. He kissed his son goodbye and held the weeping Eulalia tightly to him.

Eloy knew that the rebels were fighting a bad government. He said to himself, 'All governments are bad and I've got to serve whatever government it happens to be.' And he accepted his position fatalistically. The world was too complicated for him. 'What can I do about it?' he thought.

His lieutenant went with him to the combat zone, leading his detachment. After six exhausting days' marching they reached their objective. 'Let's hope this will soon be over,' said Eloy to his friend Private Julian, a *guajiro* like himself, while the campaign rations were being prepared in a grove of *yagruma* trees at the foot of a hillside. 'Yes. But it looks a long job ... Although they haven't got a chance against us. Not against the army ...' Eloy smiled, a little reassured. The breeze blew cool through the leaves of the *yagrumas* which sheltered them.

The mountain peaks looked very near. He could make out the vultures flying, high up, like moving black dots against a prussian blue firmament. 'Up there,' he said to himself nervously, 'that's where they are.'

At dawn they began the climb. They went forward slowly. An advance party was clearing the way. Behind them marched the main body of soldiers, in single file, well spaced out so as not to make things easy for the snipers hidden in the forest. Behind every tree trunk death was spying on them. The weary soldiers were well aware of that.

After five hours' march they pitched camp at the foot of a small hill. One of the first spells of guard duty fell to Private Eloy. He took up his post behind a rock, looking out over a valley full of palm trees and mist. In the distance he could see the sea, a fringe of pale blue. His companion on duty said, 'Not my idea of a good time, stuck here in these bushes.' 'Not mine either. I don't know what we're doing here,' answered Eloy. And they both stared at the horizon, looking for possible signs of the rebels.

At nightfall the shooting began. Nobody slept well. Shots that came from nobody knew where. Nervous guards firing. Tense nerves. At first light they continued the weary march, from mountain to mountain through dales and gorges. It was cold and drizzling. A constant mist blurred the trees. Raindrops on the leaves, mud. The soldiers chatted among themselves, 'You can't see a thing.' 'Why aren't we going down yet?' 'Why can't they send somebody else on this wild goose chase?'

At sunrise they came under heavy fire. A group of rebels suddenly blazed away at them. The leading soldiers fell, surprised by bursts of shots coming from no fixed point. Eloy saw them coming back, pale-faced and groaning. The lieutenant, revolver in hand, came up to them. 'Now it's our turn to go on ahead. Forward!' And Eloy moved into the vanguard.

A day later he went into battle. As they were going along a path between tall hollyhocks the bullets reached them. Three comrades fell. Eloy fired blindly straight ahead towards the woods. Beside him the machine-guns opened fire on an invisible enemy: the guerrillas. The lieutenant urged them on. 'Into the woods! They're in those woods!'

The soldiers advanced. At full speed. Before reaching the woods ahead several had fallen to the grass. Eloy arrived. He pushed on into the woods. Rifle ready to fire. But he couldn't see anyone. He went on.

From beside the trunk of a *yaba* tree someone spoke to him. It was a bearded man, very young. He was leaning heavily against the tree-trunk, motionless. Eloy went up to him cautiously. He saw the blood. 'I'll take him prisoner,' thought Eloy. He heaved him on to his shoulders. He didn't weigh much. He was a thin man, his uniform torn and dirty. Eloy walked a little way. He got tired. Carefully he laid the wounded man down on the grass while he got his strength back. He listened. There was no sound of shouting any more.

'I'm thirsty. Give me some water.' Eloy pointed his gun at the man's eyes. But all he saw in them was fever and helplessness. 'Water.' Eloy looked at him. It was a peasant face, like his own, a long-suffering face. The wounded man drank from the bottle Eloy handed him. 'Thanks.' 'That's all right,' said Eloy. And he did not know what to do.

'I think I'm badly hurt,' said the wounded man. 'No, no you aren't.' 'I shan't get out of this alive.' Eloy thought, 'If I take this *guajiro* prisoner he'll certainly be murdered. The lieutenant will kill him. He's already killed two *guajiros* just because they couldn't tell him where the rebels were.'

'How old are you?' 'Nineteen,' said the wounded man. Eloy thought, 'If I take him the lieutenant will kill him. I'll leave him here. Let him take his chance. Anyway he can't live long with a Springfield bullet in his stomach.'

The wounded man looked questioningly at him. He could see him thinking. He knew his fate was being decided. 'Come with us, soldier, come on ...' Eloy didn't answer. He hesitated. He didn't like the lieutenant and he didn't care for the government. Undecided, he didn't know what to do. 'Come with us,' repeated the young man. 'You carry me and I'll guide you.'

Eloy got up and said. 'I'm going to spare your life, you're a *guajiro* like me. Escape as soon as you can.' 'I can't, soldier, I can't escape. If you go, kill me, I don't want to die here – all by myself. Take me to my people and come and join the revolution.' Eloy said nothing. He turned his back on the wounded man. He walked out of the wood.

'We'd given you up,' said a soldier who was a friend of his. 'They caught us by surprise. There are two dead.'

That night none of the soldiers slept. They were expecting a surprise attack. Eloy, lying awake, thought, 'I'd go, but what about Eulalia and the boy ... And beginning to face hardships now. When I was all settled in life ... Poverty in the fields all over again ... His wound wasn't serious. Wonder if he's still alive? I ought to have killed him really, so he wouldn't suffer any more. But I couldn't have done it.'

At daybreak they were issued with rations. Eloy put aside two bananas, a tin of condensed milk, some biscuits. And at the first opportunity he slipped away into the woods.

There he was, even paler than before. He was delirious with fever. 'Here, I've brought you some biscuits and bananas and a can of milk ...' But the wounded man didn't recognise him. Eloy said to himself, 'If I carry him now I don't know where to take him. Even if I wanted to go with him now he can't guide me ...'

He found himself surrounded by rifles. The lieutenant shouted, 'Hang them both! Traitors have to be hung!' Eloy saw the ropes, the noose. He didn't try to defend himself.

When the troop turned and looked back for an instant to see if the two bodies had stopped twitching, they saw them swaying in the wind which blew down from the Sierra.

The lieutenant remarked to his shaken orderly, 'I never liked Private Eloy,' he said, scratching his eyebrow. 'He wasn't a safe man.' The orderly said nothing. They crossed a stream, its waters ruffled by the strong breeze. Its banks were covered with fine grey sand. The lieutenant knelt down at the water's edge and bathed his eyebrow where a mosquito bite had raised an irritating swelling.

Once Upon a Time

Nadine Gordimer

In a house, in a suburb, in a city, there were a man and his wife who loved each other very much and were living happily ever after. They had a little boy, and they loved him very much. They had a cat and a dog that the little boy loved very much. They had a car and a caravan trailer for holidays, and a swimming-pool which was fenced so that the little boy and his playmates would not fall in and drown. They had a housemaid who was absolutely trustworthy and an itinerant gardener who was highly recommended by the neighbours. For when they began to live happily ever after they were warned, by that wise old witch, the husband's mother, not to take on anyone off the street. They were inscribed in a medical benefit society, their pet dog was licensed, they were insured against fire, flood damage and theft, and subscribed to the local Neighbourhood Watch, which supplied them with a plaque for their gates lettered YOU HAVE BEEN WARNED over the silhouette of a would-be intruder. He was masked: it could not be said if he was black or white, and therefore proved the property owner was no racist.

It was not possible to insure the house, the swimming pool or the car against riot damage. There were riots, but these were outside the city, where people of another colour were quartered. These people were not allowed into the suburb except as reliable housemaids and gardeners, so there was nothing to fear, the husband told the wife. Yet she was afraid that some day such people might come up the street and tear off the plaque YOU HAVE BEEN WARNED and open the gates and stream in ... Nonsense, my dear, said the husband, there are police and soldiers and tear-gas and guns to keep them away. But to please her – for he loved her very much and buses were being burned, cars stoned, and schoolchildren shot by the police in those quarters out of sight and hearing of the suburb – he had electronically-controlled gates fitted. Anyone who pulled off the sign YOU HAVE BEEN WARNED and tried to open the gates would have to announce his intentions by pressing a button and speaking into a receiver relayed to the house. The little boy was fascinated by the device and used it as a walkie-talkie in cops and robbers play with his small friends.

The riots were suppressed, but there were many burglaries in the suburb and somebody's trusted housemaid was tied up and shut in a cupboard by thieves while she was in charge of her employers' house. The trusted housemaid of the man and wife and little boy was so upset by this misfortune befalling a friend left, as she herself often was, with responsibility for the possessions of the man and his wife and the little boy that she implored her employers to have burglar bars attached to the doors and windows of the house, and an alarm system installed. The wife said, She is right, let us take heed of her advice. So from every window and door in the house where they were living happily ever after they now saw

128

the trees and sky through bars, and when the little boy's pet cat tried to climb in by the fanlight to keep him company in his little bed at night as it customarily had done, it set off the alarm keening through the house.

The alarm was often answered – it seemed – by other burglar alarms, in other houses, that had been triggered by pet cats or nibbling mice. The alarms called to one another across the gardens in shrills and bleats and wails that everyone soon became accustomed to, so that the din roused the inhabitants of the suburb no more than the croak of frogs and musical gratings of cicadas' legs. Under cover of the electronic harpies' discourse intruders sawed the iron bars and broke into homes, taking away hi-fi equipment, television sets, cassette players, cameras and radios, jewellery and clothing, and sometimes were hungry enough to devour everything in the refrigerator or paused audaciously to drink the whisky in the cabinets or patio bars. Insurance companies paid no compensation for single malt, a loss made keener by the property owner's knowledge that the thieves wouldn't even have been able to appreciate what it was they were drinking,

Then the time came when many of the people who were not trusted housemaids and gardeners hung about the suburb because they were unemployed. Some importuned for a job: weeding, or painting a roof, anything, *baas*, madam. But the man and his wife remembered the warning about taking on anyone off the street. Some drank liquor and fouled the street with discarded bottles. Some begged, waiting for the man or his wife to drive the car out of the electronically-operated gates. The sat about with their feet in the gutters, under the jacaranda trees that made a green tunnel of the street – for it was a beautiful suburb, spoilt only by their presence – and sometimes they fell asleep lying right before the gates in the midday sun. The wife could never see anyone go hungry. She sent the trusted housemaid out with bread and tea, but the trusted housemaid said these were loafers and *tsotsis*, who would come and tie her up and shut her in a cupboard. The husband said, She's right. Take heed of her advice. You only encourage them with your bread and tea. They are looking for their chance … And he brought the little boy's tricycle from the garden into the house every night, because if the house was surely secure, once locked and with the alarm set, someone might still be able to climb over the wall or the electronically-closed gates into the garden.

You are right, said the wife, then the wall should be higher. And the wise old witch, the husband's mother, paid for the extra bricks as her Christmas present to her son and his wife – the little boy got a Space Man outfit and a book of fairy tales.

But every week there were more reports of intrusion: in broad daylight and the dead of night, in the early hours of the morning, and even in the lovely summer twilight – a certain family was at dinner while the bedrooms were being ransacked upstairs. The man and his wife, talking of the latest armed robbery in the suburb, were distracted by the sight of the little boy's pet cat effortlessly arriving over the seven-foot wall, descending first with a rapid bracing of extended forepaws down on the sheer vertical surface, and then a graceful launch, landing with swishing tail within the property. The whitewashed wall was marked with the cat's comings and goings: and on the street side of the wall there were larger red-earth smudges that could have been made by the kind of broken running shoes, seen on the feet of unemployed loiterers, that had no innocent destination.

When the man and wife and little boy took the pet dog for its walk round the neighbourhood streets they no longer paused to admire this show of roses or that perfect lawn: these were hidden behind an array of different varieties of security fences, walls and devices. The man, wife, little boy and dog passed a remarkable choice: there was the low-cost option of pieces of broken glass embedded in cement along the top of walls, there were iron grilles ending in lance-points, there were attempts at reconciling the aesthetics of prison architecture with the Spanish Villa style (spikes painted pink) and with the plaster urns of neo-classical facades (twelve-inch pikes finned like zig-zags of lightning and painted pure white). Some walls had a small board affixed, giving the name and telephone number of the firm responsible for the installation of the devices. While the little boy and the pet dog raced ahead, the husband and wife found themselves comparing the possible effectiveness of each style against its appearance: and after several weeks when they paused before this barricade or that without needing to speak, both came out with the conclusion that only one was worth considering. It was the ugliest but the most honest in its suggestion of the pure concentration camp style, no frills, all evident efficacy. Placed the length of walls, it consisted of a continuous coil of still and shining metal serrated into jagged blades, so that there would be no way of climbing over it and no way through its tunnel without getting entangled in its fangs. There would be no way out, only a struggle getting bloodier and bloodier, a deeper and sharper hooking and tearing of flesh. The wife shuddered to look at it. You're right, said the husband, anyone would think twice … And they took heed of the advice on a small board fixed to the wall: Consult DRAGON'S TEETH The People For Total Security.

Next day a gang of workmen came and stretched the razor-bladed coils all round the walls of the house where the husband and wife and little boy and pet dog and cat were living happily ever after. The sunlight flashed and slashed off the serrations, the cornice of razor thorns encircled the home, shining. The husband said, Never mind. It will weather. The wife said. You're wrong. They guarantee it's rust-proof. And she waited until the little boy had run off to play before she said, I hope the cat will take heed … The husband said, Don't worry, my dear, cats always look before they leap. And it was true that from that day on the cat slept in the little boy's bed and kept to the garden, never risking a try at breaching security.

One evening, the mother read the little boy to sleep with a fairy story from the book the wise old witch had given him at Christmas. Next day he pretended to be the Prince who braves the terrible thicket of thorns to enter the palace and kiss the Sleeping Beauty back to life: he dragged a ladder to the wall, the shining coiled tunnel was just wide enough for his little body to creep in, and with the first fixing of its razor-teeth in his knees and hands and head he screamed and struggled deeper into its tangle. The trusted housemaid and the itinerant gardener, whose 'day' it was, came running, the first to see and to scream with him, and the itinerant gardener tore his hands trying to get at the little boy. Then the man and his wife burst wildly into the garden and for some reason (the cat, probably) the alarm set up wailing against the screams while the bleeding mass of the little boy was hacked out of the security coil with saws, wire-cutters, choppers, and they carried it – the man, the wife, the hysterical trusted housemaid and the weeping gardener – into the house.

See Me in Me Benz and T'ing

Hazel D. Campbell

The Lady of the house sucked her teeth angrily as she put down the telephone.

'Carl knows I can't stand driving down to his factory,' she complained loudly.

'Why doesn't he just send the driver for the car!' she gestured in annoyance. 'In a hurry, my foot!'

The maid dusting the furniture nearby didn't comment as she knew her place better than that. In any case she wasn't being directly addressed.

'Don't forget the upstairs sitting room,' the Lady ordered, suddenly turning her annoyance on the maid. 'Yesterday I ran my finger over the TV up there. Absolutely filthy! Don't know why it's so difficult to get you people to do an honest day's work.'

Carl had absolutely ruined her day, the Lady pouted. She would be late for the session with the girls and miss all the nice gossip. Furthermore Carl knew that she hated driving through the section of the city where he worked. So much violence, and all those people glaring at her in hostility as if she were personally responsible for the squalor in which they lived. Like wild animals some of them with their uncombed heads and crazy talk. Watching her as if any minute they would attack. No wonder the papers were always full of horrible stories about them. Now she wouldn't even have time to do her nails and she had so wanted to show off the new shade Sylvia had brought back from Miami for her. Damn that Carl!

Quarrelling with the maid, the gardener and the two Alsatians blocking her path to the car, she gathered her purse and her keys and got into the sleek black Status Symbol which had been resting in the double carport.

The 4.5 litre, V8 engine sprang alive and settled into a smooth purr before she eased into reverse, turned it around and put it into drive to make the long trip from home on the hilltop to workplace by the seashore. It gathered speed as she rolled down hill, and, as always, she felt a tiny moment of panic at the strength of the horsepower growling softly under the bonnet, controlled only by the swift movement of foot from accelerator to brake as necessary. Carl had promised her this car if ever he was able to buy a newer one, but since 1972, no new models had been allowed into the island so she had to be content with the Mazda, which didn't satisfy her vanity half as much as the Status Symbol did.

Annoyance returned sharply as she imagined how the girls would have exclaimed when she drove up in the Benz.

' Eh! Eh! How you manage get Carl to part with his car?' they would tease. And she would explain that the Mazda was in the garage so she had to borrow the Benz, pretending with them that it was these great big problems which made life so difficult. Then they would settle down to a nice chat about the Number of Things they were having to do without! And Who had just gone, or Who had decided to! And pass a pleasant hour or so laughing at the kinds of things some people were packing into trailers. And had they heard that Jonesie was working in a shoe store in Miami as a sales clerk! No! God forbid! And *my dearing*, and *oh dearing* each other, they would with large eyes contemplate life in the 70s in Jamaica, each realizing, but not saying that they did not know how to come to grips with it.

As the Lady skirted the Sealand trailer parked at the foot of the hill, she remembered that she wanted to renew her campaign to get Carl to migrate. After all he could even pack the factory machinery in the trailer, she thought, and they could relocate in Florida. Lots of other people were doing it. Things were really getting impossible. Imagine, not even tampons in the shops. Good thing she knew many people who were still commuting between America and Jamaica, so she could get a ready supply of the things she absolutely couldn't do without.

As she passed through Half-Way-Tree, the Lady collected her wandering thoughts. She would need all her concentration to get safely through the congested parts of the city she would soon be entering. Just last week a friend of theirs had been pulled from his car and savagely beaten because he had scraped somebody's motorcycle with the car.

She made sure all the doors were locked, touched the power button for the windows and turned on the air-conditioning. She was always grateful for the ability to lock up herself in the car. Lock out the stenches of gutters and overcrowded human flesh. Lock out the sounds of human distress. From the cool, slight dimness of the red interior of the Status Symbol, even the sight of distress took on a sort of unreal appearance, so she could pass through uncontaminated.

A little past Half-Way-Tree, she hesitated a moment before deciding to turn down Maxfield Avenue. She hated cutting across Spanish Town Road, but this way was shorter, and Carl had said to hurry. That was why he hadn't sent somebody for the car. The double journey would take too long. She had wasted enough time already, so she would have to hurry. She was afraid of Carl's bad temper. He would lash out at her even in front of the factory staff if he was sufficiently annoyed. She was sure it wasn't all that important for him to get the car. Probably some luncheon or other for which he needed the Status Symbol to impress somebody. He wouldn't dream of driving one of the small company cars. Not him. No matter how it inconvenienced her.

By the time she reached the first set of lights, the traffic had already begun to crawl. Not much use her ability to move from 0 to 60 miles per hour in ten seconds flat, here. Not much use all that horse power impatiently ticking under her restraining foot. Thank God for the air-conditioning, she thought again.

As she waited for the green light, the billboard on top of the shop at the corner caught her eye. 'LIFE IS A MUTUAL AFFAIR' it read. Somebody ought to tell Carl that. Instead of dragging her through this horrid part of town he should be protecting her. Any moment now a bullet could shatter the glass and kill her.

She spent a moment indulging her overactive imagination, seeing her blood-splattered breast and she leaning back as still as she had seen a body in some film or other. The impatient horn behind her made her suddenly realize that the lights had changed.

She moved off quickly, smiling at her melodramatic thoughts. Actually she wasn't feeling too afraid. After all, didn't Carl do this trip everyday? And if there were problems outside, she couldn't hear.

That group of people milling around outside that shop, for instance, she couldn't see what was creating the excitement and since she couldn't hear either, what did it matter? They were like puppets in a silent movie. In fact she could not decide what they were doing. Was it a dead man they were looking at?

Christ! Her imagination! She really must do something about it, she thought. Wonder if she was getting off. Lots of people getting crazy these days, because of all the stress and strain, she'd heard. They were probably just fassing in somebody's business as usual, idle bitches, that they were. Look at those on that other piazza. Winding up themselves and gyrating to some beat loud enough to penetrate her castle of silence. That's all they were good for. And those others milling around the betting shop, race forms in hand. How could the country progress with so many idlers never wanting to do any work? And even those who said they worked couldn't do a thing. Her annoyance deepened as she thought how she couldn't get Miriam to clean the bathrooms properly. No amount of telling did the trick. No matter how often she told her what to do. No matter what amount of cleaning things she bought.

The traffic began to crawl again as she neared Spanish Town Road. Just at the part she would have liked to pass over quickly. Now she had plenty of time to look out through her smoky glass at unreality.

Another billboard. Advertising Panther. Good-looking youth, she thought. Not like the dirty bums cotching up the walls, the street posts, and any fence strong enough to bear their weight. The Panther boy looked like somebody who would care about life and not spawn too many children. But what did he have to do with these dirty creatures passing as men around the place? Giving all those worthless women thousands of children by the minute. Silly ad, she thought. Silly place to put it.

Ah! There was her favourite on the other side. Beautiful clouds and a jet taking off into the sunset – FASTEST WAY TO CANADA – She liked to think about that. Escape from the closing-in feeling of Jamaica. It was only a matter of time, her friends were saying, before all of Kingston and St Andrew looked like these dumps around her. Zinc fences hiding poverty and nastiness, hate and crime. Smells she could only imagine now. People living, no, not living, existing on top of each other. God forbid that she should ever live like that. That she should even live close to this. Bad enough to have to drive through.

Suddenly she realized that none of the cars was moving,

neither up nor down, and that there was an unusual amount of people on the streets even for this crowded area.

What could be the matter? she thought in alarm.

Then she noticed the driver in front of her turning up his car windows in haste, seconds before she saw the first part of the crowd running between the cars. Running in her direction.

Oh God! She prayed softly. Had it finally happened? Were they going to get her? Stories she had heard about riots and those who got caught in them raced through her thoughts.

But even in her panic she still felt fairly safe. Wasn't she protected in her air-conditioned car? People were swarming around like the cartoon figures on Spider Man, the TV show her children were always watching. And she was looking on at the action, as if she were in a drive-in movie, with a larger-than-life screen surrounding her. But even as she watched, the sounds of their distress began to filter into her castle.

She wondered what was happening, but dared not open her window to find out. To do that would be to let in reality which would force her to think and act. Better to stay locked up in the car and hope that whatever it was would allow her to get moving soon.

In the distance she saw something like a wisp of smoke and thought perhaps it might be a fire. But why would the people be running away from it? And why did they look so frightened?

And even as she noticed their fright it turned to anger

right before her eyes. One minute they were running away from something, wave after wave of them. The next, like a freeze in a movie, a pause, long enough to allow anger to replace fright. A turn around. And then hell breaking loose.

She could tell by the shape of their mouths that they were angry. By their swoops for weapons that they were angry.

From nowhere, it seemed, sticks, stones and bottles appeared and began to fly around.

The car, she panicked. They would scratch the car, and what would Carl say? That the damn ducoman wouldn't match the shade and he would have to do over the whole car – if there was any duco available? Funny how Carl's anger about a scratched car was more real to her than the anger of the mass of people milling around about her, getting hurt, hurting and going mad with anger for what reason she didn't even know.

The traffic going in the opposite direction had somehow managed to move on, and those behind her were frantically trying to turn around to escape the mob.

The Lady tense and nervous put the car into reverse and put her finger on the horn hoping that they would clear the way for her to turn around. But all she did was to bring down their wrath on her. The reality of their anger began to reach her when she felt the human earthquake rocking the car. A human earthquake fed by anger. Anger now turned against the Status Symbol in their midst. The out-of-place Symbol.

142

The driver before her had abandoned his car. The doors were wide open with people like ants tearing off the wings of an injured beetle. Oh God! There was one of the mad men trying to open her door to pull her out. To destroy her. She didn't need to hear them yelling, 'Mash it up! Mash it up!' She shut her eyes in pain as the shattering sound reached her and the stone which had smashed the windscreen settled on the seat beside her, letting in reality. The reality of angry sounds, angry smells, demented faces and nightmare hands grabbing her.

She didn't hear herself screaming as they dragged her from the car, roughly discarding her to fight as best she could. They weren't interested in her. Only in the Symbol. The Symbol must be destroyed. The insulting Symbol, black as their bodies, inside red as their blood.

Mash it up! Not just a scratch. Damage it beyond repair. Rip out its red heart. Turn it over. And just to make sure, set it on fire. Destroy it forever.

The Lady stood in the crowd, assaulted by forgotten humanity, and she still didn't feel their reality. She was remembering the day her husband had brought the car home. The first year the factory had made a profit he had ordered this car to celebrate. *'This is the symbol, baby,'* he'd said. *'The symbol that we've arrived.'* That was why, between them, they jokingly referred to it as the Status Symbol.

Her feelings now were tied up with the Symbol's destruction. Her blood scattered in the streets. Her flesh being seared by the fire. And the sudden roar of the flames as the Symbol caught fire, pulled a scream of animal rage from the very bowels of her.

But the roar of the sacrifice quieted the mob's anger. As quickly as they had come they began to melt away.

The Lady didn't notice. The Lady didn't hear herself bawling. Neither did she feel the gentle hands of the two old women steering her away from the scene of her destruction.

'Thank God is only the car!' they whispered, as they hurried her away from the street, down a lane and into a yard. They took her behind one of the zinc fences, into the safety of their humanity. 'Sometimes the people them not so fortunate,' they murmured as they bathed her cuts and bruises and gave her some sweet sugar and water to drink. 'You is lucky is only this happen to you.'

And they didn't ask her name. For them it wasn't important who she was. She needed help and they gave what they could without question, fear or favour.

Five Hours to Simla

Anita Desai

Then, miraculously, out of the pelt of yellow fur that was
the dust growing across the great northern Indian plain, a
wavering grey line emerged. It might have been a cloud
bank looming, but it was not – the sun blazed, the earth
shrivelled, the heat burnt away every trace of spring's
beneficence. Yet the grey darkened, turned bluish, took on
substance.

'Look – mountains!'

'Where?'

'I can't see any mountains.'

'Are you blind? Look, look up – not down, fool!'

A scuffle broke out between the boys on the sticky grime
of the Rexine-covered front seat. It was quietened by a tap
on their heads from their mother in the back. 'Yes, yes,
mountains. The Himalayas. We'll be there soon.'

'Huh.' A sceptical grunt from the driver of the tired,
dust-buried grey Ambassador car. 'At least five more
hours to Simla.' He ran his hand over the back of his neck
where all the dirt of the road seemed to have found its way
under the wilting cotton collar.

'Sim-la! Sim-la!' the boys set up a chant, their knees
bouncing up and down in unison.

Smack, the driver's left hand landed on the closest pair,
bringing out an instant stain of red and sudden, sullen
silence.

'Be quiet!' the mother hissed from the back unnecessarily.

The Ambassador gave a sudden lurch, throwing everyone forwards. The baby, whose mouth had been glued to the teat of a bottle like a fly to syrup, came unstuck and wailed with indignation. Even their mother let out a small involuntary cry. Her daughter, who had been asleep on the back seat, her legs across her mother's lap, now stirred.

'Accident!' howled the small boy who had been smacked, triumphantly.

But it was not. His father had stopped just short of the bicycle rickshaw ahead, which had just avoided running into the bullock cart carrying farmers' families to market. A bus, loaded with baggage and spilling over with passengers, had also ground to a halt with a shrieking of brakes. Ahead of it was a truck, wrapped and folded in canvas sheets that blocked all else from sight. The mountains had disappeared and so had the road.

After the first cacophony of screeching brakes and grinding gears, there followed the comparatively static hum of engines, and drivers waited in exasperation for the next lurch forwards. For the moment there was a lull, curious on that highway. Then the waiting very quickly began to fray at the edges. The sun was beating on the metal of the vehicles, and the road lay flattened across the parched plain, with no trees to screen it from the sun. First one car horn began to honk, then a bicycle rickshaw began to clang its bell, then a truck blared its musical horn, and then the lesser ones began to go pom-pom, pom-pom almost in harmony, and suddenly, out of the centre of all that noise, a long, piercing wail emerged.

The two boys, the girl, the baby, all sat up, shocked. More so when they saw what their father was doing. Clenching the wheel with both hands, his head was lowered on to it, and the blare of the horn seemed to issue out of his fury.

The mother exclaimed.

The father raised his head and banged on the wheel, struck it. 'How will we get to Simla before dark?' he howled.

The mother exclaimed again, shocked. 'But we'll be moving again in a minute.'

As if to contradict her, the driver of the truck stalled at the top of the line, swung himself out of the cabin into the road. He'd turned off his engine and stood in the deeply rutted dust, fumbling in his shirt pocket for cigarettes.

Other drivers got out of and down from their vehicles: the bullock-cart driver lowered himself from the creaking cart; the bicycle-rickshaw driver descended; the bus driver got out and stalked, in his sweat-drenched khakis, towards the truck driver standing at the head of the line; and they all demanded, 'What's going on? Breakdown?'

The truck driver watched them approach but was lighting his cigarette and didn't answer. Then he waved an arm – his movements were leisurely, elegant, quite unlike what his driving had been – and said, 'Stone throw. Somebody threw a stone. Hit windshield. Cracked it.'

The father in the Ambassador had also joined them in the road. Hands on his hips, he demanded, 'So?'

'So?' said the truck driver, narrowing his eyes. They were grey in a tanned face, heavily outlined and elongated with kohl, and his hair was tied up in a bandanna with a long loose end that dangled upon his shoulder. 'So we won't be moving again till the person who did it is caught, and a *faisla* is made – a settlement.'

Immediately a babble broke out. All the drivers flung out their hands and arms in angry, demanding gestures, their voices rose in questioning, in cajoling, in argument. The truck driver stood looking at them, watching them, his face inscrutable. Now and then he lifted the cigarette to his mouth and drew a deep puff. Then abruptly he swung around, clambered back into the cabin of his truck and started the engine with a roar at which the others fell back, their attitudes slackening in relief, but then he wheeled the truck around and parked it squarely across the highway so no traffic could get past in either direction. The highway at that point had narrowed to a small culvert across a dry stream-bed full of stones. Now he clambered up the bank of the culvert and sat down, his legs wide apart in their loose and not too clean pyjamas, regarding the traffic piling up in both directions as though he was watching sheep filing into a pen.

The knot of drivers in the road began to grow, joined by many of the passengers demanding to know the cause of this impasse.

'Dadd-ee! Dadd-ee!' the small boys yelled, hanging out of the door their father had left open and all but falling out into the dust. 'What's happened, Dadd-ee?'

'Shut the door!' their mother ordered sharply but too late. A yellow pye-dog came crawling out of the shallow ditch that ran alongside the road and, spying an open door, came slinking up to it, thin, hairless tail between its legs, eyes showing their whites, hoping for bread but quite prepared for a blow instead.

The boys drew back on seeing its exploring snout, its teeth bared ready for a taste of bread. 'Mad dog!' shouted one. 'Mad dog!' bellowed the other.

'Shh!' hissed their mother.

Since no one in the car dared drive away a creature so dangerous, someone else did. A stone struck its ribs, and with a yelp it ducked under the car to hide, but already the next beggar was at the door, throwing himself in with much the same mixture of leering enquiry and cringing readiness to withdraw. 'Bread,' he whined, stretching out a bandaged hand. 'Paisa, paisa. Mother, mother,' he pleaded, seeing the mother cower in her seat with the baby. The children cowered too.

They knew that if they remained thus for long enough and made no move towards purse or coin, he would leave: he couldn't afford to waste too much time on them when there were so many potential donors lined up so conveniently along the highway. The mother stared glassily ahead through the windscreen at the heat beating off the metal bonnet. The children could not tear their eyes away from the beggar – his sores, his bandages, his crippled leg, the flies gathering …

When he moved on, the mother raised a corner of her

sari to her mouth and nose. From behind it she hissed: 'Shut-the-door!'

Unsticking their damp legs from the moist, adhesive seat, the boys scrambled to do so. As they leaned out to grab the door however, and the good feel of the blazing sun and the open air struck at their faces and arms, they turned around to plead, 'Can we get out? Can we go and see what's happening?'

So ardent was their need that they were about to fall out of the open door when they saw their father detaching himself from the knot of passengers and drivers standing in the road and making his way back to them. The boys hastily edged back until he stood leaning in at the door. The family studied his face for signs; they were all adept at this, practising it daily over the breakfast table at home, and again when he came back from work. But this situation was a new one, a baffling one: they could not read it, or his position on it.

'What's happening? the mother asked faintly at last.

'Damn truck driver,' he swore through dark lips. 'Some boy threw a rock – probably some goatherd in the field – and cracked his windscreen. He's parked the truck across the road, won't let anyone pass till there's a *faisla*. Says he won't move till the police come and get him compensation. Stupid damn fool – what compensation is a goatherd going to pay, even if they find him?'

The mother leaned her head back. What had reason to do with men's tempers? she might have asked. Instead, she sighed, 'Is there a policeman?'

150

'What – here? In this forsaken desert?' her husband retorted, drawing in harsh breaths of overheated, dust-laden air as if he were breathing in all the stupidity around him. He could see passengers climbing down from the bus and the bullock cart, climbing across the ditch into the fields, and fanning out – some to lower their trousers, others to lift their saris behind the thorn bushes. If the glare was not playing tricks with his eyes, he thought he saw a puff of dust in the distance that might have been raised by goats' hooves.

'Take me to see, Dadd-ee, take me to see,' the boys had begun to clamour, and to their astonishment he stood aside and let them climb out and even led them back to the truck that stood imperviously across the culvert.

The mother opened and shut her mouth silently. Her daughter stood up and hung over the front seat to watch the disappearing figures. In despair, she cried, 'They're gone!'

'Sit down! Where can they go?'

'I want to go too, Mumm-ee, I want to go too-oo.'

'Be quiet. There's nowhere to go.'

The girl began to wail. It was usually a good strategy in a family with loud voices, but this time her grievance was genuine: her head ached from the long sleep in the car, from the heat beating on its metal top, from the lack of air, from the glare and from hunger. 'I'm hung-gree,' she wept.

'We were going to eat when we reached Solan,' her mother reminded her. 'There's such a nice-nice restaurant at the railway station in Solan. Such nice-nice omelettes they make there.'

'I want an omelette!' wailed the child.

'Wait till we get to Solan.'

'When will we reach it? *When*?'

'Oh, I don't know. Late. Sit down and open that basket at the back. You'll find something to eat there.'

But now that omelettes at Solan had been mentioned the basket packed at home with Gluco biscuits and potato chips held no attraction for the girl. She stopped wailing but sulked instead, sucking her thumb, a habit she was supposed to have given up but which resurfaced for comfort when necessary.

She did not need to draw upon her thumb juices for long. The news of the traffic jam on the highway had spread. From somewhere – it seemed from nowhere for there was no village bazaar, market place or stall visible in that dusty dereliction – wooden barrows came trundling along towards the waiting traffic, bearing freshly cut lengths of sugar cane; bananas already more black than yellow from the sun that baked them; peanuts in their shells roasting in pans set on embers. Men, women and children were climbing over the ditch like phantoms, materializing out of the dust, with baskets on their heads filled not only with food but with amusements as well – a trayload of paper toys painted indigo and violent pink, small bamboo pipes that released rude noises and a dyed feather on a spool. Kites, puppets, clay carts, wooden toys and tin whistles. The vendors milled around the buses, cars and rickshaws, and were soon standing at their car window, both vocally and manually proffering goods for sale.

The baby let drop its narcotic rubber teat, delighted. Its eyes grew big and shone at all it saw flowering about it. The little girl was perplexed, wondering what to choose from so much till the perfect choice presented itself in a rainbow of colour: green, pink and violet, her favourites. It was a barrow of soft drinks, and nothing on this day of gritty dust, yellow sun and frustrating delay could be more enticing than those bottles filled with syrups in those dazzling floral colours which provoked in her a scream of desire.

'Are you mad?' her mother said promptly. 'You think I'll let you drink a bottle full of typhoid and cholera germs?'

The girl gasped with disbelief at being denied. Her mouth opened wide to issue a protest, but her mother went on, 'After you have your typhoid-and-cholera injection, you may. You want a nice, big typhoid-and-cholera injection first?'

The child's mouth was still open in contemplation of the impossible choice when her brothers came plodding back through the dust, each carrying a pith-and-bamboo toy – a clown that jounced upon a stick and a bird that whirled upon a pin. Behind them the father slouched morosely. He had his hands deep in his pockets, and his face was lined with a frown deeply embedded with dust.

'We'll be here for hours,' he informed his wife through the car window. 'A rickshaw driver has gone off to the nearest *thana* to find a policeman who can put sense into that damn truck driver's thick head.' Despondently he threw himself into the driver's seat and sprawled there. 'Must be a hundred and twenty degrees,' he sighed.

'Pinky, where is the water bottle? Pass the water bottle to Daddy,' commanded the mother solicitously.

He drank from the plastic bottle, tilting his head back and letting the water spill into his mouth. But it was so warm it was hardly refreshing, and he spat the last mouthful out of the car window into the dust. A scavenging chicken alongside the tyre skipped away with a squawk.

All along the road, in the stationary traffic, drivers and passengers were searching for shade, for news, for some sign of release. Every now and then someone brought information on how long the line of cars and trucks now was. Two miles in each direction was the latest estimate, at least two miles.

Up on the bank of the culvert the man who had caused it all sat sprawling, his legs wide apart. He had taken off his bandanna, revealing a twist of cotton wool dipped in fragrant oil that was tucked behind his ear. He had bought himself a length of sugar cane and sat chewing it, ripping off the tough outer fibre with strong flashing teeth, then drawing the sweet syrup out of its soft white inside and spitting out, with relish, the pale fibre sucked dry. He seemed deliberately to spit in the direction of those who stood watching in growing frustration.

'Get hold of that fellow! *Force* him to move his truck,' somebody suddenly shouted out, driven to the limit of his endurance. 'If he doesn't, he'll get the thrashing of his life.'

'Calm down, Sirdarji,' another placated him with a light laugh to help put things back in perspective. 'Cool down. It's hot, but you'll get your cold beer when you get to Solan.'

'When will that be? When my beard's gone grey?'

'Grey hair is nothing to be ashamed of,' philosophized an elder who had a good deal of it to show. 'Grey hair shows patience, forbearance, a long life. That is how to live long – patiently, with forbearance.'

'And when one has work to do, what then?' the Sikh demanded, rolling up his hands into fists. The metal bangle on his wrist glinted.

'Work goes better after a little rest,' the elder replied, and demonstrated by lowering himself on to his haunches and squatting there on the roadside like an old bird on its perch or a man waiting to be shaved by a roadside barber. And, like an answer to a call, a barber did miraculously appear, an itinerant barber who carried the tools of his trade in a tin box on his head. No one could imagine where he had emerged from, or how far he had travelled in search of custom. Now he squatted and began to unpack a mirror, scissors, soap, blades, even a small rusty cigarette tin full of water. An audience stood watching his expert moves and flourishes and the evident pleasure these gave the elder.

Suddenly the truck driver on the bank waved a hand

and called, 'Hey, come up here when you've finished. I could do with a shave too – and my ears need cleaning.'

There was a gasp at his insolence, and then indignant protests.

'Are you planning to get married over there? Are we not to move till your bride arrives and the wedding is over?' shouted someone.

This had the wrong effect: it made the crowd laugh. Even the truck driver laughed. He was somehow becoming a part of the conspiracy. How had this happened?

In the road, the men stood locked in bafflement. In the vehicles, the tired passengers waited. 'Oo-oof,' sighed the mother. The baby, asleep as if stunned by the heat, felt heavy as lead in her arms. 'My head is paining, and it's time to have tea.'

'Mama wants tea, mama wants tea!' chanted her daughter, kicking at the front seat.

'Stop it!' her father snapped. 'Where is the kitchen? Where is the cook? Am I to get them out of the sky? Or is there a well filled with tea?'

The children all burst out laughing at the idea of drawing tea from a well, but while they giggled helplessly, a *chai* wallah did appear, a tray with glasses on his head, a kettle dangling from his hand, searching for the passenger who had called for tea.

There was no mention of cholera or typhoid now. He was summoned, glasses were filled with milky, sweet tea and handed out, the parents slurped thirstily, and the children stared, demanding sips, then flinching from the scalding liquid.

Heartened, the father began to thrash around in the car, punch the horn, stamp ineffectually on the accelerator. 'Damn fool,' he swore. 'How can this happen? How can this be allowed? Only in this bloody country. Where else can one man hold up four miles of traffic?'

Handing back an empty glass, the mother suggested, 'Why don't you go and see if the policeman's arrived?'

'Am I to go up and down looking for a policeman? Should I walk to Solan to find one?' the man fumed. His tirade rolled on like thunder out of the white blaze of the afternoon. The children listened, watched. Was it getting darker? Was a thundercloud approaching. Was it less bright? Perhaps it was evening. Perhaps it would be night soon.

'What will we do when it grows dark?' the girl whimpered. 'Where will we sleep?'

'Here, on the road!' shouted the boys. 'Here on the road!' Their toys were long since broken and discarded. They needed some distraction. Their sister could easily be moved to tears by mentioning night, jackals, ghosts that haunt highways, robbers who carry silk handkerchiefs to strangle their victims ...

Suddenly, one of the drivers, hitching up his pyjamas and straightening his turban, came running back towards the stalled traffic, shouting, 'They're moving! The policeman's come! They'll move now! There'll be a *faisla*!'

Instantly the picture changed from one of discouragement, despair and approaching darkness to animation, excitement, hope. All those loitering in the road leaped back into their vehicles, and in a moment the air was filled with the roar of revving engines as with applause.

The father too was pressing down on the accelerator, beating upon the steering wheel, and the children settling into position, all screaming, 'Sim-la! Sim-la!' in unison.

But not a single vehicle moved an inch. None could. The obstructing truck had not been moved out of the way. The driver still sprawled on the bank, propped up on one elbow now, demanding of the policeman who had arrived, 'So? Have you brought me compensation? NO? Why not? I told you I would not move till I received compensation. So where is it? Hah? What is the *faisla*? Hah?'

The roar of engines faltered, hiccuped, fell silent. After a while, car doors slammed as drivers and passengers climbed out again. Groups formed to discuss the latest development. What was to be done now? The elder's philosophical patience was no longer entertained. No one bandied jokes with the villain on the bank any more. Expressions turned grim.

Suddenly the mother wailed, 'We'll be here all night,' and the baby woke crying: it had had enough of being confined in the suffocating heat; it wanted air, it wanted escape. All the children began to whine. The mother drew herself up. 'We'll have to get something to eat,' she said and called over to her husband standing in the road, 'Can't you get some food for the children?'

He threw her an irritated look over his shoulder. Together with the men in the road, he was going back to the culvert to see what could be done. There was an urgency about their talk now, their suggestions. Dusk had begun to creep across the fields like a thicker, greyer layer of dust. Some of the vendors lit kerosene lamps on their barrows, so small and faint that they did nothing but accentuate the darkness. Some of them were disappearing over the fields, along paths visible only to them, having sold their goods and possibly having a long way to travel. All that could be seen in the dark were the lighted pinpricks of their cigarettes.

What the small girl had most feared did now happen – the long, mournful howl of a jackal lifted itself out of the stones and thorn bushes and unfurled through the dark towards them. While she sat mute with fear, her brothers let out howls of delight and began to imitate the invisible creature's call,

The mother was shushing them fiercely when they heard the sound they had given up hope of hearing: the sound of a moving vehicle. It came roaring up the road from behind them – not at all where they had expected – overtaking them in a cloud of choking dust. Policemen in khaki, armed with steel-tipped canes, leaned out of it, their moustaches bristling, their teeth gleaming, eyes flashing and ferocious as tigers. And the huddled crowd stranded on the roadside fell aside like sheep; it might have been they who were at fault.

But the police truck overtook them all, sending them

hurriedly into the ditch for safety, and drew up at the culvert. Here the police jumped out, landing with great thuds on the asphalt, and striking their canes hard upon it for good measure. The truck's headlights lit up the bank with its pallid wash.

Caught in that illumination, the truck driver rose calmly to his feet, dusted the seat of his pyjamas, wound up the bandanna round his head, all in one fluid movement, and without a word leaped lightly back into the driver's seat of his truck. He turned the key, started the engine, manoeuvred into an onward position and, while his audience held its disbelieving breath, set off towards the north.

After a moment they saw that he had switched on his lights. He had also turned on his radio, and a song could be heard.

> Father, I am leaving your roof,
> To my bridegroom's home I go …

His tail lights could be seen dwindling in the dark. The police swung around, flourishing their canes. 'Get on! *Chalo!*' they bellowed. '*Chalo, chalo*, get on, all of you,' and they did.

Coffee for the Road

Alex la Guma

They were past the maize-lands and driving through the wide, low, semi-desert country that sprawled away on all sides in reddish brown flats and depressions. The land, going south, was scattered with scrub and thorn bushes, like a vast unswept carpet. Far to the right, the metal vanes of a windmill pump turned wearily in the faint morning breeze, as if it had just been wakened to set reluctantly about its duty of sucking water from the miserly earth. The car hurtled along the asphalt road, its tyres roaring along the black surface.

'I want another sandwich, please,' Zaida said. She huddled in the blanketed space among the suitcases in the back. She was six years old and weary from the long, speeding journey, and her initial interest in the landscape had evaporated, so that now she sagged tiredly in the padded space, ignoring the parched gullies and stunted trees that whisked past.

'There's some in the tin. You can help yourself, can't you?' the woman at the wheel said, without taking her eyes off the road. 'Do you want to eat some more, too, Ray?'

'Not hungry any more,' the boy beside her replied. He was gazing out at the barbed-wire fence that streamed back outside the turned-up window.

'How far's it to Cape Town, Mummy?' Zaida asked, munching a sandwich.

'We'll be there tomorrow afternoon,' the woman said.

'Will Papa be waiting?'

'Of course.'

'There's some sheep,' the boy, Ray, said. A scattering of farm buildings went by, drab, domino-shaped structures along a brown slope.

The mother had been driving all night and she was fatigued, her eyes red, with the feeling of sand under the lids, irritating the eyeballs. They had stopped for a short while along the road, the night before; parked in a gap off the road outside a small town. There had been nowhere to put up for the night: the hotels were for Whites only. In fact, only Whites lived in these towns and everybody else, except for the servants, lived in tumbledown mud houses in the locations beyond. Besides, they did not know anybody in this part of the country.

Dawn had brought depression, gloom, ill-temper, which she tried to control in the presence of the children. After having parked on that stretch of road until after midnight, she had started out again and driven, the children asleep, through the rest of the night.

Now she had a bad headache, too, and when Zaida said, 'Can I have a meatball, Mummy?' she snapped irritably: 'Oh, dash it all! It's there, eat it, can't you?'

The landscape ripped by, like a film being run backwards, red-brown, yellow-red, pink-red, all studded with sparse bushes and broken boulders. To the east a huge outcrop of rock strata rose abruptly from the arid earth, like a titanic wedge of purple-and-lavender-layered

162

cake topped with chocolate-coloured boulders. The car passed over a stretch of gravel road and the red dust boiled behind it like a flame-shot smoke-screen. A bird, its long, ribbon-like tail streaming behind it, skimmed the brush beyond the edge of the road, flitting along as fast as the car.

'Look at that funny bird, Mummy,' the boy, Ray, cried, and pressed his face to the dust-filmed glass.

The mother ignored him, trying to relax behind the wheel, her feet moving unconsciously, but skilfully, on the pedals in the floor. She thought that it would have been better to have taken a train, but Billy had written that he'd need the car because he had a lot of contacts to visit. She hoped the business would be better in the Cape. Her head ached, and she drove automatically. She was determined to finish the journey as quickly as possible.

Ray said, 'I want some coffee.' And he reached for the thermos flask on the rack under the dashboard. Ray could take care of himself, he did not need to have little things done for him.

'Give me some, too,' Zaida called from the back, among the suitcases.

'Don't be greedy,' Ray said to her. 'Eating, eating, eating.'

'I'm not greedy. I want a drink of coffee.'

'You had coffee this morning.'

'I want some more.'

'Greedy. Greedy.'

Children,' the mother said wearily, 'children, stop that arguing.'

'He started first,' Zaida said.

'Stop it. Stop it,' the mother told her.

Ray was unscrewing the cap of the thermos. When it was off he drew the cork and looked in. 'Man, there isn't any,' he said. 'There isn't any more coffee.'

'Well, that's just too bad,' the mother said.

'I want a drink,' Zaida cried. 'I'm thirsty, I want some coffee.'

The mother said wearily: 'Oh, all right. But you've got to wait. We'll get some somewhere up the road. But wait, will you?'

The sun was a coppery smear in the flat blue sky, and the countryside, scorched yellow and brown, like an immense slice of toast, quivered and danced in the haze. The woman drove on, tiredly, her whole mind rattling like a stale nut. Behind the sunglasses her eyes were red-rimmed and there was a stretched look about the dark, handsome, Indian face. Her whole system felt taut and stretched like the wires of a harp, but too tight so that a touch might snap any one of them.

The miles purred and growled and hummed past: flat country and dust-coloured *koppies*, the baked clay *dongas* and low ridges of hills. A shepherd's hut, lonely as a lost soul, crouched against the shale-covered side of a flat hill; now and then a car passed theirs, headed in the opposite direction, going north, crashing by in a shrill whine of slip-stream. The glare of the sun quivered and quaked as if the air was boiling.

'I want some coffee,' Zaida repeated petulantly. 'We didn't have no coffee.'

'We'll buy some coffee,' her mother told her. 'We'll buy some for the road as soon as we get to a café. Stop it, now. Eat another sandwich.'

'Don't want sandwich. Want coffee.'

A group of crumbling huts, like scattered, broken cubes passed them in a hollow near the road and a band of naked, dusty brown children broke from the cover of a sheep-pen, dashing to the side of the road, cheering and waving at the car. Ray waved back, laughing, and then they were out of sight. The wind-scoured metal pylon of a water-pump drew up and then disappeared too. Three black men trudged in single file along the roadside, looking ahead into some unknown future, wrapped in tattered, dusty blankets, oblivious of the heat, their heads shaded by the ruins of felt hats. They did not waver as the car spun past them but walked with fixed purpose.

The car slowed for a steel-slung bridge and they rumbled over the dry, rock-strewn bed of a stream. A few sheep, their fleeces black with dust, sniffed among the boulders, watched over by a man like a scarecrow.

At a distance, they passed the coloured location and then the African location, hovels of clay and clapboard strewn like discoloured dice along a brown slope, with tiny people and ant-like dogs moving among them. On another slope the name of the town was spelled out in whitewashed boulders.

The car passed the sheds of a railway siding, with the sheep milling in corrals, then lurched over the crossing and bounced back on to the roadway. A Coloured man went by on a bicycle, and they drove slowly past the nondescript brown front of the Railway Hotel, a line of stores, and beyond a burnt hedge a group of white men with red, sun-skinned, wind-honed faces sat drinking at tables in front of another hotel with an imitation Dutch-colonial façade. There was other traffic parked along the dusty, gravel street of the little town: powdered cars and battered pick-up trucks, a wagon in front of a feed store. An old Coloured man swept the pavement in front of a shop, his reed broom making a hissing sound, like gas escaping in spurts.

Two white youths, pink-faced and yellow-haired, dressed in khaki shirts and shorts, stared at the car, their eyes suddenly hostile at the sight of a dark woman driving its shiny newness, metal fittings factory-smooth under the film of road dust. The car spun a little cloud behind it as it crept along the red-gravel street.

'What's the name of this place, Mummy?' the boy, Ray, asked. 'I don't know,' the mother replied, tired, but glad to be able to slow down. 'Just some place in the Karroo.'

'What's the man doing?' Zaida asked, peering out through the window.

'Where?' Ray asked, looking about. 'What man?'

'He's gone now,' the little girl said. 'You didn't look quickly.' Then, 'Will we get some coffee now?'

'I think so,' the mother said. 'You two behave yourselves and there'll be coffee. Don't you want a cool drink?'

'No,' the boy said. 'You just get thirsty again, afterwards.'

'I want a lot of coffee with lots of sugar,' Zaida said.

'All right,' the mother said. 'Now stop talking such a lot.'

Up ahead, at the end of a vacant lot, stood a café. Tubular steel chairs and tables stood on the pavement outside, in front of its shaded windows. Its front was decorated with old Coca Cola signs and painted menus. A striped awning shaded the tables. In the wall facing the vacant space was a foot-square hole where non-Whites were served, and a group of ragged Coloured and African people stood in the dust and tried to peer into it, their heads together, waiting with forced patience.

The mother drove the car up and brought it to a stop in front of the café. Inside a radio was playing and the slats of the venetian blinds in the windows were clean and dustless.

'Give me the flask,' the mother said, and took the thermos bottle from the boy. She unlatched the door. 'Now, you children, just sit quiet. I won't be long.'

She opened the door and slid out and, standing for a moment on the pavement, felt the exquisite relief of loosened muscles. She straightened body. But her head still ached badly and that spoiled the momentary delight which she felt. With the feeling gone, her brain was tired again and the body once more a tight-wound spring. She straightened the creases out of the smart tan suit she was wearing but left the jacket unbuttoned. Then, carrying the thermos flask, she crossed the sidewalk, moving between the plastic-and-steel furniture into the café.

Inside, the café was cool and lined with glass cases

displaying cans and packages like specimens in some futuristic museum.

From somewhere at the back of the place came the smell and sound of potatoes being fried. An electric fan buzzed on a shelf and two gleaming urns, one of tea and the other of coffee, steamed against the back wall.

The only other customer was a small white boy with tow-coloured hair, a face like a near-ripe apple and a running nose. He wore a washed-out print shirt and khaki shorts, and his dusty bare feet were yellow-white and horny with cracked callouses. His pink, sticky mouth explored the surface of a lollipop while he scanned the covers of a row of outdated magazines in a wire rack.

Behind the glass counter and a trio of soda fountains a broad, heavy woman in a green smock thumbed through a little stack of accounts, ignoring the group of dark faces pressing around the square hole in the side wall. She had a round-shouldered, thick body and reddish-complexioned face that looked as if it had been sand-blasted into its component parts: hard plains of cheeks and knobbly cheek-bones and a bony ridge of nose that separated twin pools of dull grey; and the mouth a bitter gash, cold and malevolent as a lizard's, a dry, chapped and serrated pink crack.

She looked up and started to say something, then saw the colour of the other woman and, for a moment, the grey pools of the eyes threatened to spill over as she gaped. The thin pink mouth writhed like a worm as she sought for words.

'Can you fill this flask with coffee for me, please?' the mother asked.

The crack opened and a screech came from it, harsh as the sound of metal rubbed against stone. 'Coffee? My Lord Jesus Christ!' the voice screeched. 'A bedamned *coolie* girl in here!' The eyes started in horror at the brown, tired, handsome Indian face with its smart sunglasses, and the city cut of the tan suit. 'Coolies, Kaffirs and Hottentots outside,' she screamed. 'Don't you bloody well know? And you talk *English,* too, hey!'

The mother stared at her, startled, and then somewhere inside her something went off, snapped like a tight-wound spring suddenly loose, jangling shrilly into action, and she cried out with disgust as her arm came up and the thermos flask hurtled at the white woman.

'Bloody white trash!' she cried. 'Coolie yourself!'

The flask spun through the air and, before the woman behind the counter could ward it off, it struck her forehead above an eyebrow, bounced away, tinkling as the thin glass inside the metal cover shattered. The woman behind the counter screeched and clapped a hand to the bleeding gash over her eye, staggering back. The little boy dropped his lollipop with a yelp and dashed out. The dark faces at the square hatch gasped. The dark woman turned and stalked from the café in a rage.

She crossed the sidewalk, her brown face taut with anger and opened the door of her car furiously. The group of non-Whites from the hole in the wall around the side of the building came to the edge of the vacant lot and stared at her as she slammed the door of the car and started the motor.

She drove savagely away from the place, her hands gripping the wheel tightly, so that the knuckles showed yellow through the brown skin. Then she recovered herself and relaxed wearily, slowing down, feeling tired again, through her anger. She took her time out of town while the children gazed, sensing that something was wrong.

Then the boy, Ray, asked, 'Isn't there any coffee, Mummy? And where's the flask?'

'No, there isn't any coffee,' the mother replied. 'We'll have to do without coffee, I'm afraid.'

'I wanted coffee,' the little girl, Zaida, complained.

'You be good,' the mother said. 'Mummy's tired. And please stop chattering.'

'Did you lose the flask?' Ray asked.

'Keep quiet, keep quiet,' the woman told him, and they lapsed into silence.

They drove past the edge of the town, past a dusty service station with its red pumps standing like sentinels before it. Past a man carrying a huge bundle of firewood on his head, and past the last buildings of the little town: a huddle of whitewashed cabins with chickens scrabbling in the dooryard, a sagging shearing-shed with a pile of dirty bales of wool inside, and a man hanging over a fence, watching them go by.

The road speared once more into the yellow-red-brown countryside and the last green trees dwindled away. The sun danced and jiggled like a midday ghost across the expressionless earth, and the tyres of the car rumbled faintly on the black asphalt. There was some traffic ahead of them but the woman did not bother to try to overtake.

The boy broke the silence in the car by saying, 'Will Papa take us for drives?'

'He will, I know,' Zaida said. 'I like this car better than Uncle Ike's.'

'Well, *he* gave us lots of rides,' Ray replied. 'There goes one of those funny birds again.'

'Mummy, will we get some coffee later on?' Zaida asked.

'Maybe, dear. We'll see,' the mother said.

The dry and dusty landscape continued to flee past the window on either side of the car. Up ahead the sparse traffic on the road was slowing down and the mother eased her foot on the accelerator.

'Look at that hill,' the boy, Ray, cried. 'It looks like a face.'

'Is it a real face?' Zaida asked, peering out.

'Don't be silly,' Ray answered. 'How can it be a real face? It just *looks* like a face.'

The car slowed down and the mother, thrusting her head through her window, peered forward past the car in front and saw the roadblock beyond it.

A small riot-van, a Land Rover, its windows and spotlight screened with thick wire mesh, had been pulled up half-way across the road, and a dusty automobile parked opposite to it, forming a barrier with just a car-wide space between them. A policeman in khaki shirt, trousers and flat cap leaned against the front fender of the automobile and held a Sten-gun across his thighs. Another man in khaki sat at the wheel of the car, and a third policeman stood by the gap, directing the traffic through after examining the drivers.

The car ahead slowed down as it came up to the gap, the driver pulled up and the policeman looked at him, stepped back and waved him on. The car went through, revved and rolled away.

The policeman turned towards the next car, holding up a hand, and the mother driving the car felt the sudden pounding of her heart. She braked and waited, watching the khaki-clad figure strolling the short distance towards her.

He had a young face, with the usual red-burned complexion of the land, under the shiny leather bill of the cap. He was smiling thinly but the smile did not reach his eyes which bore the hard quality of chips of granite. He wore a holstered pistol at his waist and, coming up, he turned towards the others and called, 'This looks like the one.'

The man with the Sten-gun straightened but did not come forward. His companion inside the car just looked across at the woman.

The policeman in the road said, still smiling slightly: 'Ah, we have been waiting for you. You didn't think they'd phone ahead, hey?'

The children in the car sat dead still, staring, their eyes troubled. The mother said, looking out: 'What's it all about?'

'Never mind what's it all about,' the policeman said to her. '*You* know what it's all about.' He looked her over and nodded. '*Ja*, darkie girl with brown suit and sunglasses. You're under arrest.'

'What's it all about?' the woman asked again. Her voice was not anxious, but she was worried about the children.

'Never mind. You'll find out,' the policeman told her coldly. 'One of those agitators making trouble here. Awright, listen.' He peered at her with flint-hard eyes. 'You turn the car around and don't try no funny business, hey? Our car will be in front and the van behind, so watch out.' His voice was cold and threatening.

'Where are you taking us? I've got to get my children to Cape Town.'

'I don't care about that,' he said. 'You make trouble here then you got to pay for it.' He looked back at the police car and waved a hand. The driver of the police car started it up and backed and then turned into the road.

'You follow that motor car,' the policeman said. 'We're going back that way.'

The woman said nothing but started her own car, manoeuvring it until they were behind the police car.

'Now don't you try any funny tricks,' the policeman said again. She stared at him and her eyes were also cold now. He went back to the riot-truck and climbed in. The car in front of her put on speed and she swung behind it, with the truck following.

'Where are we going, Mummy?' asked Zaida.

'You be quiet and behave yourselves,' the mother said, driving after the police car.

The countryside, red-brown and dusty, moved past them: the landscapes they had passed earlier now slipping the other way. The blue sky danced and wavered and the parched, scrub-strewn scenery stretched away around them in the yellow glare of the sun.

'I wish we had some coffee,' the little girl, Zaida, said.

The Day Mr Prescott Died

Sylvia Plath

It was a bright day, a hot day, the day old Mr Prescott died. Mama and I sat on the side seat of the rickety green bus from the subway station to Devonshire Terrace and jogged and jogged. The sweat was trickling down my back, I could feel it, and my black linen was stuck solid against the seat. Every time I moved it would come loose with a tearing sound, and I gave Mama an angry 'so there' look just like it was her fault, which it wasn't. But she only sat with her hands folded in her lap, jouncing up and down, and didn't say anything. Just looked resigned to fate is all.

'I say, Mama,' I'd told her after Mrs Mayfair called that morning, 'I can see going to the funeral even though I don't believe in funerals, only what do you mean we have to sit up and watch with them?'

'It is what you do when somebody close dies,' Mama said, very reasonable. 'You go over and sit with them. It is a bad time.'

'So it is a bad time,' I argued. 'So what can I do, not seeing Liz and Ben Prescott since I was a kid except once a year at Christmas time for giving presents at Mrs Mayfair's. I am supposed to sit around hold handkerchiefs, maybe?'

With that remark, Mama up and slapped me across the mouth, the way she hadn't done since I was a little kid and very fresh. 'You are coming with me,' she said in her dignified tone that means definitely no more fooling.

So that is how I happened to be sitting in this bus on the hottest day of the year. I wasn't sure how you dressed for waiting up with people, but I figured as long as it was black it was all right. So I had on this real smart black linen suit and a little veil hat, like I wear to the office when I go out to dinner nights, and I felt ready for anything.

Well, the bus chugged along and we went through the real bad parts of East Boston I hadn't seen since I was a kid. Ever since we moved to the country with Aunt Myra, I hadn't come back to my home town. The only thing I really missed after we moved was the ocean. Even today on this bus I caught myself waiting for that first stretch of blue.

'Look, Mama, there's the old beach,' I said, pointing.

Mama looked and smiled. 'Yes.' Then she turned around to me and her thin face got very serious. 'I want you to make me proud of you today. When you talk, talk. But talk nice. None of this fancy business about burning people up like roast pigs. It isn't decent.'

'Oh, Mama,' I said, very tired. I was always explaining. 'Don't you know I've got better sense. Just because old Mr Prescott had it coming. Just because nobody's sorry, don't think I won't be nice and proper.'

I knew that would get Mama. 'What do you mean nobody's sorry?' she hissed at me, first making sure people weren't near enough to listen. 'What do you mean talking so nasty?'

'Now, Mama,' I said, 'you know Mr Prescott was twenty years older than Mrs Prescott and she was just waiting for

176

him to die so she could have some fun. Just waiting. He was a grumpy old man even as far back as I remember. A cross word for everybody and he kept getting that skin disease on his hands.'

'That was a pity the poor man couldn't help,' Mama said piously. 'He had a right to be crotchety over his hands itching all the time, rubbing them the way he did.'

'Remember the time he came to Christmas Eve supper last year?' I went on stubbornly. 'He sat at the table and kept rubbing his hands so loud you couldn't hear anything else, only the skin like sandpaper flaking off in little pieces. How would you like to live with *that* every day?'

I had her there. No doubt about it, Mr Prescott's going was no sorrow for anybody. It was the best thing that could have happened all around.

'Well,' Mama breathed, 'we can at least be glad he went so quick and easy. I only hope I go like that when my time comes.'

Then the streets were crowding up together all of a sudden, and there we were by old Devonshire Terrace and Mama was pulling the buzzer. The bus dived to a stop, and I grabbed hold of the chipped chromium pole behind the driver just before I would have shot out the front window. 'Thanks, mister,' I said in my best icy tone, and minced down from the bus.

'Remember,' Mama said as we walked down the sidewalk, going single file where there was a hydrant, it was so narrow, 'remember, we stay as long as they need us. And no complaining. Just wash dishes, or talk to Liz, or whatever.'

'But Mama,' I complained, 'how can I say I'm sorry about Mr Prescott when I'm really not sorry at all? When I really think it's a good thing?'

'You can say it is the mercy of the Lord he went so peaceful,' Mama said sternly. 'Then you will be telling the honest truth.'

I got nervous only when we turned up the little gravel drive by the old yellow house the Prescotts owned on Devonshire Terrace. I didn't feel even the least bit sad. The orange-and-green awning was out over the porch, just like I remembered, and after ten years it didn't look any different, only smaller. And the two poplar trees on each side of the door had shrunk, but that was all.

As I helped Mama up the stone steps onto the porch, I could hear a creaking and sure enough, there was Ben Prescott sitting and swinging on the porch hammock like it was any other day in the world but the one his Pop died. He just sat there, lanky and tall as life. What really surprised me was he had his favorite guitar in the hammock beside him. Like he'd just finished playing 'The Big Rock Candy Mountain', or something.

'Hello Ben,' Mama said mournfully. 'I'm so sorry.'

Ben looked embarrassed. 'Heck, that's all right,' he said. 'The folks are all in the living-room.'

I followed Mama in through the screen door, giving Ben a little smile. I didn't know whether it was all right to smile because Ben was a nice guy, or whether I shouldn't, out of respect for his Pop.

Inside the house, it was like I remembered too, very dark so you could hardly see, and the green window blinds didn't help. They were all pulled down. Because of the heat or the funeral, I couldn't tell. Mama felt her way to the living-room and drew back the portières. 'Lydia?' she called.

'Agnes?' There was this little stir in the dark of the living-room and Mrs Prescott came out to meet us. I had never seen her looking so well, even though the powder on her face was all streaked from crying.

I only stood there while the two of them hugged and kissed and made sympathetic little noises to each other. Then Mrs Prescott turned to me and gave me her cheek to kiss. I tried to look sad again but it just wouldn't come, so I said, 'You don't know how surprised we were to hear about Mr Prescott.' Really, though, nobody was at all surprised, because the old man only needed one more heart attack and that would be that. But it was the right thing to say.

'Ah, yes,' Mrs Prescott sighed. 'I hadn't thought to see this day for many a long year yet.' And she led us into the living-room.

After I got used to the dim light, I could make out the people sitting around. There was Mrs Mayfair, who was Mrs Prescott's sister-in-law and the most enormous woman I've ever seen. She was in the corner by the piano.

Then there was Liz, who barely said hello to me. She was in shorts and an old shirt, smoking one drag after the other. For a girl who had seen her father die that morning, she was real casual, only a little pale is all.

Well, when we were all settled, no one said anything for a minute, as if waiting for a cue, like before a show begins. Only Mrs Mayfair, sitting there in her layers of fat, was wiping away her eyes with a handkerchief, and I was reasonably sure it was sweat running down and not tears by a long shot.

'It's a shame,' Mama began then, very low, 'It's a shame, Lydia, that it had to happen like this. I was so quick in coming I didn't hear tell who found him even.'

Mama pronounced 'him' like it should have a capital H, but guessed it was safe now that old Mr Prescott wouldn't be bothering anybody again, with that mean temper and those raspy hands. Anyhow, it was just the lead that Mrs Prescott was waiting for.

'Oh, Agnes,' she began, with a peculiar shining light to her face, 'I wasn't even here. It was Liz found him, poor child.'

'Poor child,' sniffed Mrs Mayfair into her handkerchief. Her huge red face wrinkled up like a cracked watermelon. 'He dropped dead right in her arms he did.'

Liz didn't say anything, but just ground out one cigarette only half smoked and lit another. Her hands weren't even shaking. And believe me, I looked real carefully.

'I was at the rabbi's,' Mrs Prescott took up. She is a great one for these new religions. All the time it is some new minister or preacher having dinner at her house. So now it's a rabbi, yet. 'I was at the rabbi's, and Liz was home getting dinner when Pop came home from swimming. You know the way he always loved to swim, Agnes.'

Mama said yes, she knew the way Mr Prescott always loved to swim.

'Well,' Mrs Prescott went on, calm as this guy on the Dragnet program, 'it wasn't more than eleven-thirty. Pop always liked a morning dip, even when the water was like ice, and he came up and was in the yard drying off, talking to our next door neighbor over the hollyhock fence.'

'He just put up that very fence a year ago,' Mrs Mayfair interrupted, like it was an important clue.

'And Mr Gove, this nice man next door, thought Pop looked funny, blue, he said, and Pop all at once didn't answer him but just stood there staring with a silly smile on his face.'

Liz was looking out of the front window where there was still the sound of the hammock creaking on the front porch. She was blowing smoke rings. Not a word the whole time. Smoke rings only.

'So Mr Gove yells to Liz and she comes running out, and Pop falls like a tree right to the ground, and Mr Gove runs to get some brandy in the house while Liz holds Pop in her arms ...'

'What happened then?' I couldn't help asking, just the way I used to when I was a kid and Mama was telling burglar stories.

'Then,' Mrs Prescott told us, 'Pop just ... passed away,

right there in Liz's arms. Before he could even finish the brandy.'

'Oh, Lydia,' Mama cried. 'What you have been through!'

Mrs Prescott didn't look as if she had been through much of anything. Mrs Mayfair began sobbing in her handkerchief and invoking the name of the Lord. She must have had it in for the old guy, because she kept praying, 'Oh, forgive us our sins,' like she had up and killed him herself.

'We will go on,' Mrs Prescott said, smiling bravely. 'Pop would have wanted us to go on.'

'That is all the best of us can do,' Mama sighed.

'I only hope I go as peacefully,' Mrs Prescott said.

'Forgive us our sins,' Mrs Mayfair sobbed to no one in particular.

At this point, the creaking of the hammock stopped outside and Ben Prescott stood in the doorway, blinking his eyes behind the thick glasses and trying to see where we all were in the dark. 'I'm hungry,' he said.

'I think we should all eat now,' Mrs Prescott smiled on us. 'The neighbors have brought over enough to last a week.'

'Turkey and ham, soup and salad,' Liz remarked in a bored tone, like she was a waitress reading off a menu. 'I just didn't know where to put it all.'

'Oh, Lydia,' Mama exclaimed, 'Let *us* get it ready. Let *us* help. I hope it isn't too much trouble ...'

'Trouble, no,' Mrs Prescott smiled her new radiant smile. 'We'll let the young folks get it.'

Mama turned to me with one of her purposeful nods and I jumped up like I had an electric shock. 'Show me where the things are, Liz,' I said, 'and we'll get this set up in no time.'

Ben tailed us out to the kitchen, where the black old gas stove was, and the sink, full of dirty dishes. First thing I did was pick up a big heavy glass soaking in the sink and run myself a long drink of water.

'My, I'm thirsty,' I said and gulped it down. Liz and Ben were staring at me like they were hypnotised. Then I noticed the water had a funny taste, as if I hadn't washed out the glass well enough and there were drops of some strong drink left in the bottom to mix with the water.

'That,' said Liz after a drag on her cigarette, 'is the last glass Pop drank out of. But never mind.'

'Oh Lordy, I'm sorry,' I said, putting it down fast. All at once I felt very much like being sick because I had a picture of old Mr Prescott, drinking his last from the glass and turning blue. 'I really am sorry.'

Ben grinned 'Somebody's got to drink out of it someday.' I liked Ben. He was always a practical guy when he wanted to be.

Liz went upstairs to change then, after showing me what to get ready for supper.

'Mind if I bring in my guitar?' Ben asked, while I was starting to fix up the potato salad.

'Sure, it's okay by me,' I said. 'Only won't folks talk? Guitars being mostly for parties and all?'

'So let them talk. I've got a yen to strum.'

I made tracks around the kitchen and Ben didn't say much, only sat and played these hillbilly songs very soft, that made you want to laugh and sometimes cry.

'You know, Ben,' I said, cutting up a plate of cold turkey, 'I wonder, are you really sorry.'

Ben grinned, that way he has. 'Not really sorry, now, but I could have been nicer. Could have been nicer, that's all.'

I thought of Mama, and suddenly all the sad part I hadn't been able to find during the day came up in my throat. 'We'll go on better than before,' I said. And then I quoted Mama like I never thought I would: 'It's all the best of us can do.' And I went to take the hot pea soup off the stove.

'Queer, isn't it,' Ben said. 'How you think something is dead and you're free, and then you find it sitting in your own guts laughing at you. Like I don't feel Pop has really died. He's down there somewhere inside of me, looking at what's going on. And grinning away.'

'That can be the good part,' I said, suddenly knowing that it really could. 'The part you don't have to run from. You know you take it with you, and then when you go any place, it's not running away. It's just growing up.'

Ben smiled at me, and I went to call the folks in. Supper was kind of a quiet meal, with lots of good cold ham and turkey. We talked about my job at the insurance office, and I even made Mrs Mayfair laugh, telling about my boss Mr Murray and his trick cigars. Liz was almost engaged,

Mrs Prescott said, and she wasn't half herself unless Barry was around. Not a mention of old Mr Prescott.

Mrs Mayfair gorged herself on three desserts and kept saying 'Just a sliver, that's all. Just a sliver!' when the chocolate cake went round.

'Poor Henrietta,' Mrs Prescott said, watching her enormous sister-in-law spooning down ice cream. 'It's that psychosomatic hunger they're always talking about. Makes her eat so.'

After coffee which Liz made on the grinder, so you could smell how good it was, there was an awkward little silence. Mama kept picking up her cup and sipping from it, although I could tell she was really all through. Liz was smoking again, so there was a small cloud of haze around her. Ben was making an airplane glider out of his paper napkin.

'Well,' Mrs Prescott cleared her throat, 'I guess I'll go over to the parlor now with Henrietta. Understand, Agnes, I'm not old-fashioned about this. It said definitely no flowers and no one needs to come. It's only a few of Pop's business associates kind of expect it.'

'I'll come,' said Mama staunchly.

'The children aren't going,' Mrs Prescott said. 'They've had enough already.'

'Barry's coming over later,' Liz said. 'I have to wash up.'

'I will do the dishes,' I volunteered, not looking at Mama. 'Ben will help me.'

'Well, that takes care of everybody, I guess.' Mrs Prescott

helped Mrs Mayfair to her feet, and Mama took her other arm. The last I saw of them, they were holding Mrs Mayfair while she backed down the front steps, huffing and puffing. It was the only way she could go down safe, without falling, she said.

From Brooklyn to Karachi via Amsterdam

S. Afzal Haider

My cousin Azra who lives in a basement apartment in Manhattan gave me a contraption for catching mice. It was a cardboard box which, when folded in the prescribed method, assembled into a miniature igloo with a single entrance. The inside bottom was covered with a thick, sticky, glue-like substance that shone like glossy polyurethane on a dark oak floor, rather like the one in the dining room of my own house.

I used the trap one time. I found the mouse still alive, anchored to the shiny floor just out of reach of the bit of bread I'd used for bait. It made desperate chirping noises as it craned its neck forward trying to reach the bread. I didn't like this method of entrapment, alive and stuck, nourishment just out of reach.

I put the igloo in a white plastic bag from Lucky's Grocery Store, tied it with a green wire twist and dropped it into the garbage can outside my house. I wondered how long it took a mouse to suffocate. They don't collect garbage until Thursday on my block, and it was only Monday.

It is Thursday evening, just before dinner. The six o'clock news flickers without sound as I learn from my brother through international tele-communication that Baba's ill health has taken a turn for the worse. Asif is a doctor, a professor of pathology. 'His mind is fine,' Asif tells me in his clinical voice, 'but he is refusing to listen, he doesn't want to eat or drink and he won't take his medication. He's going to slip into coma any time now.' Baba has been dying for over three years now. There is a tumour on his bladder which bleeds through a sore on his back.

Three years ago while visiting me in Brooklyn – his last visit – he saw a doctor at my insistence. He refused to have the recommended surgery. He did not like, he explained to me, the idea of the blood transfusion, his own blood mingled with that of strangers who might drink alcohol or eat pork.

I couldn't look him in the eyes. I growled, 'People are having heart transplants these days and you're worrying about a blood transfusion.'

He smiled and asked me to sit beside him on the bed. He kissed my forehead and rubbed his silver beard against my cheek and said, 'I would consider a brain transplant if necessary, but no thanks, I want to die with my own blood pumping through my own heart.'

Later in Karachi he refused the surgical treatment again, telling Asif that he couldn't bear the idea of being chemically put to sleep. 'What if the surgeon is having a bad day and performs a lobotomy by mistake while I'm out?' He added, 'A man dies only once. I want to die wide awake, with my eyes open.'

'If you want to see him, says Asif, 'you ought to come immediately.'

I don't know what to say. I ask to speak to Baba.

'You should,' says Asif. 'He likes you better and he listens to you.' I want to protest but I know it's not the right time and besides both know it's true. There is a long wait while the phone is brought to Baba, a wait filled with the clicks and chirps of transcontinental communication. They are lonely sounds, unanswered in the vast impersonal distance that lies between the two telephones. I wonder if Baba really is going to die this time.

'How are you?' I ask when Baba comes on the line.

'Pretty bad,' he says. What I admire most in my old man is his courage, even when he is afraid.

'I hear you're not eating or drinking anything,' I tell him.

'Yes,' he anwers, 'I cannot.'

'Why not?' I demand.

'My gums have shrunk and my dentures don't hold. I can't chew anything, I can't get up and go to the bathroom. I've been sick long enough. It's time to go.'

'Baba–,' against my own good rational sense, I am becoming angry.

'I can no longer paint,' Baba continues in the same soft voice, full of the calm of reason. 'I am tired of thinking about things I can do nothing about. All men die,' he says. 'All men die.'

'I'm going to leave tonight. I'll be there on Saturday morning,' I tell him with my voice breaking. 'I want to see you.'

'I want to see you too, dear boy, but I don't like being trapped in my own body, unable to move.' I remember the

189

mouse. I plead with him. 'Please eat and take your medication. I still have a lot to talk to you about.' I always tell him that. 'I don't want to find you in a coma when I arrive.'

'I can't promise, but please come.' His soft voice is weak.

I hate overseas phone calls. They are always about bad news. When I return to the dinner table the six o'clock news is over and my food has gone cold.

'Did Baba die?' asks Sean as I carry my plate to the microwave.

I have been speaking in Urdu so the entire conversation has been lost to them – them being my Forest Park, Illinois-born oriental wife Virginia, our four-year-old son, Sean, and infant daughter, Sarina.

Last year alone I travelled twice from Brooklyn to Karachi to visit my ailing father. At the end of each visit I wondered if I'd ever see him again, where I'd be when he died. My mother used to be big on weddings and funerals. 'Parents should arrange weddings for their children,' she said, 'and children should bury their parents.' I married a woman of my own choosing and missed my mother's funeral – the fate of the transplanted person. The least I can do is bury my father.

'Did Baba die?' Sean asks again.

'No,' I answer, 'but he may die any day.'

'What if Baba dies on my birthday?'

'Then we can celebrate a birth and mourn a death on the same day.' I sit down at the table again and look at

Virginia. She is burping Sarina on her shoulder and she looks back at me, waiting.

'I am going to leave tonight,' I say. 'If I make the right connections, I can be there in twenty-four hours.'

'What if your plane crashes?' Sean asks.

I begin to put food in my mouth. I have no idea what I'm eating. My wife's excellent cooking is as devoid of taste as styrofoam. I reach over to tousle my son's hair. 'What if it doesn't?' I laugh.

'What if it does?' Sean insists. 'Planes do crash. I don't want you to die.'

'When I die, I shall be extraordinarily ancient with a long white beard down to here. You will be grown up with a family of your own and you won't need your old man anymore.' I look my son straight in the eye when I tell him this. I hope I'm right.

That night I leave for Karachi via Amsterdam. I am due to arrive in Karachi on Saturday morning. As I try to fall asleep on the plane, exhausted and tired, I think of Baba and how as a little boy I always hoped he would come home at night before I fell asleep; that I would be up in the morning before he was gone for the day.

Before my family migrated to Pakistan, we lived in a small town in India, on the banks of the River Jumna. In the summertime, early on Sunday mornings, Baba woke me with kisses on my forehead and a rub of his unshaven beard on my cheeks. Before sunrise, my mother, who prayed faithfully five times a day, went to *Fajr* (morning prayers), but Baba and I set out on our fish hunt. His gun in its case across his shoulder, his hunting bag secured to the rear carrier of his bicycle, dark hair combed neatly back, dressed in a loose white shirt and trousers, he sat me on the crossbar and pedalled the long uphill route with an urgency.

We always arrived at the bank of the Jumna just as the sun rose. Baba parked the bike carefully on its stand and began the ritual which never varied: the gun was removed from its case, the single barrel, ball and muzzle loader cleaned with a ramrod. Then black powder, a homemade lead bullet and a piece of rag were packed in. I would stand at the edge of the river, watching him aim at bubbles bouncing like pearls to the surface of the water. Baba would cock the gun, put a cap on the nipple, aim and fire. Then he would lay the gun aside, place his glasses carefully next to it, kick off his sandals and jump into the water. For a few moments it was as though the river swallowed him up. I would search the surface with my eyes, knowing he would appear again but anxious none the less.

Suddenly he would split the water with a great splash and climb the bank with a fish in his hands, the river streaming from his body, his brown face shining in the sun. My father was a sure shot. He thought there was nothing in life that couldn't be undone. With our fish filleted and packed in the hunting bag, we would sail downhill toward home. Baba smoothly pedalling the bike, a strong forearm on either side of me, his cool wet white shirt flapping against my head, to Mama's Sunday morning breakfast.

Baba was an art master at Sarsuti Part Shalla, the local Hindu high school. He made his living painting portraits of famous people and common folk. A Gandhi for a Mohan Das, a Jinnah for a Mohammad Ali, and someone's deceased mother when commissioned. He wore eyeglasses that he needed to take off to see what was directly in front of him. I would watch him for hours as, in slow motion, he observed his subject through his spectacles. When he was ready to paint, he took them off. 'People wear their lives on their faces,' Baba used to say. 'To see what a person has lived, you have only to read his face.' I saw a bit of his face in each portrait he painted. Sometimes I look into a mirror and see my father looking back.

Baba gave me the most he could. Unlike my mother, he hardly ever prayed, not even on big holidays, but he read the Koran every day. Upon my departure for higher education in America, he gave me his Holy Koran. 'Read it for peace of the soul,' he admonished. It sits on a bookshelf now, unread. Baba was a generous man, but he wouldn't permit me to wear his shoes, not even his house slippers. He was a complicated man. My mother would tell him about mischief I had accomplished during the day and he would reply that it was too late, I'd already done it. Knowing the pattern of my daily difficulties, Mama would inform him what I was about to do. He replied, 'It's premature, he's done nothing yet.'

During the British Raj, Baba shaved daily with a 7 O'Clock brand blade. He wore gabardine suits, silk ties and a grey felt hat. He smoked Passing Show cigarettes. On the package was a picture of a man with a brown face wearing a grey felt hat. Folks around us called him *Sahib*; his friends called him *Kala* (black) *Sahib. Kala Sahib* enjoyed good food, dressed well, and I, having read his *Kama Sutra*, could guess what he did for good sex. 'The art of loving is in knowing your own state of arousal,' he said. 'The cuckoo should not call before it is the hour.'

Flying against time, I arrive on Saturday morning at 11:05. When I step off the plane I collide with heat so intense it feels like violent physical assault. I have an instant of panic as I realize that my years in northern latitudes have finally robbed me of the ability to tolerate my native climate. A large delegation of relatives meets me at the gate. Even before we speak, I can see from the faces of Asif and my sister, Rashida, that I am too late.

I ride with Asif in his almond green Morris Minor, listening to Urdu songs on the radio. We proceed directly to the graveyard and Asif finds a bit of shade to park in near the entrance. As another car full of relatives pulls up next to us, I look around, stiff from travel and lack of sleep, enervated by the heat, and feel the smallest tugging lift of spirit.

I love graveyards in this part of the world. They are like a carnival or a baseball park during a game, alive and full of people. Vendors by the gates sell flowers, rose water, incense, Coca Cola. Inside, people are resting, reading the Koran, burning incense, chanting prayers aloud or praying silently. Asif buys a large bottle of rose water, a package of incense and a clear plastic bag full of red rose petals. My cousin Farook buys seeds to feed the birds. The three of us, along with Rashida and her children, Adnan and Naheed, and Asif's son Habib, named after our father, make our way toward the family plot. Farook rubs his eyes with his fists and says that Baba was more like a father to him than his own father.

At our feet is the new grave: my father, the brown face in the grey felt hat, *Kala Sahib*. Someone begins the prayers for the dead. I sit down between the graves of my parents, one smoothed and benign, the other, fresh, raw, a ragged wound that has not yet scabbed over. I'm wearing Levis, a western shirt and Adidas and I'm soaked with sweat. I listen to Farook chant *Sura Al Fatiha: 'Praise be to Allah, Lord of the Creation ... King of Judgement Day.'* I pick at tiny clumps of dirt, crushing them with my fingers. My mother once expressed her fear that some day I would be unable to recite even a silent prayer for her. She was right: both my heart and my mouth are dumb.

Rashida sits next to me, holding my hand, sobbing openly. I want to cry, but I can't, or perhaps my whole body weeps as the salt of my perspiration pours out, drenching my clothes and hair so that I cannot tell the difference between my sister's tears and my own sweat.

'Tell me about Baba,' I say.

Rashida turns her face away from me and stares out at

where her children are moving among the graves. She says, 'He was sitting up in bed when you spoke with him. He looked very grey. I wrung out a towel in cool water and bathed his face. Then I helped him to lie flat. He was shivering. That frightened me more than anything else, his shivering. The heat was really bad, worse than today. The floors were so hot I was afraid the children's feet would blister. And Baba lay there shivering.'

My sister closes her eyes and presses the end of her veil over her mouth. I look down at her hand lying in mine, the familiar structure of bone and tendon under rich brown skin, a delicate, fragile-looking hand, a lie of a hand, because it contains the strength to have done those things for Baba all alone when I was far away.

'I covered him up with a cotton quilt – the one printed with grey leaves and white flowers that you gave him the first time he visited you in America. He lay there quietly with his eyes open on the single bed, next to the bed where our mother slept. I'd been sleeping in it for the past week. I wondered what people think about when they are dying. I picked up his Koran and sat down next to him. I read aloud, you know, *Sura Al Rahman*, he always liked that.'

It is The Merciful who has taught the Koran. He created man and taught him articulate speech ... which of your Lord's blessings would you deny? I remembered it well.

'Then,' Rashida goes on, 'he asked for *Sura Ya Sin*. His voice was very strong. Do you remember, *Ya Sin, I swear by the wise Koran that you are sent upon a straight path ...?*'

I nod.

'I started to cry, but I wouldn't let myself. I finished: *'Glory be to Him Who has control of all things. To Him you shall return.'* When I stopped reading, his eyes were closed. I knew then he was dying. He opened his eyes and looked up at me.

'All men should be blessed with a daughter,' he said.

I squeeze her hand. 'A daughter like you,' I tell her.

She says, 'A tear rolled down my cheek and dropped onto his beard. I don't think he noticed. He was frowning as if he were trying to remember something, then his face relaxed and he smiled. At that moment, oh, I wish you could have seen him—he might have passed for his old self.'

Yes, I think, the man in the grey felt hat. In my mind's eye I see my sister's tear sink into Baba's beard like an uncut diamond into the fine ash of a spent fire.

'He said then, "Go now, please. I am ready to sleep." I kissed him and left the room.' There are a few moments of silence as Rashida labours for control. Finally she says, 'At dawn on Friday as you were somewhere over the Atlantic, I heard the muezzin call out from the mosque, "Prayer is better than sleep." Baba did not waken for *Fajr*.'

I close my eyes and continue to hold Rashida's hand. Baba died on *Al-Jumma*, the day of congregation, under the portrait of our mother he painted when she was a young woman. He had been bathed, groomed and wrapped in a white cotton shroud. After Friday congregation in the mosque, funeral prayers were offered. In one-hundred-seventeen degrees, he was buried the same afternoon.

Rashida gets up to join her children. I sit in silence as Asif scatters a handful of rose petals on Baba's grave. He, Rashida and Farook, my nieces and nephews, move on to the other graves in the family plot, chanting prayers for the dead. Habib sprinkles rose water, Adnan and Naheed cast rose petals. I turn to my mother's grave, thinking of Camus's Monsieur Meursault and his vigil beside his mother's coffin. I too do not feel any sadder today than any other day.

My mother has been here long enough to have a name plate. I gather a handful of the rose petals scattered by the children. They are already curled and fading. Dust blows in my face and I close my eyes. Even this hot breeze, a draft from some circle of hell where the rootless and homeless wander, feels good against my wetness. I see my mother's face, red in the sun, smiling at me. There is the mole on her cheek that I had forgotten. Silently I repeat the prayers for the dead. My brother lights a few sticks of incense. I stand up, easing the stiffness from my legs, rubbing the rose petals between my palms. I open my hands; the crushed petals and their wisp of fragrance fly away with the blowing dust. As we drive through the noisy, crowded streets toward Baba's house, Asif tells me that one reason he never went abroad was to spare our mother the shock of losing both her sons. That was kind of him, I think, noble, even. 'Are you happy?' I ask.

'Am I happy?' Asif repeats. 'I am well accomplished. Daughters are happy when they become mothers. Sons always have to fight the battles of their fathers.'

I ran from my father's battles when I was eighteen, never to return to live with him, not even for high holidays.

The next morning is cloudy and dark, blanketed with heat and humidity. Perhaps it will rain, I think with hope, but by noon the wind picks up and blows away the clouds. The temperature climbs to one-hundred-twelve in the shade. I spend all that day and the next in Baba's room, cleaning out his closet, looking at his papers. There are awards and certificates (Drawing Master of Merit, Artist of Distinction), his membership in the Royal Drawing Society of London, yellowed invitations to high teas with dukes, banquets with shahs. I feel a swelling of pride and admiration: this was a grand man, my old man – my dead old man. Among his letters is a ribbon-tied bundle from an internationally renowned artist who lives in Lancaster, England. He had sought out Baba during his travels to India. There are also letters from Faye Dincin of San Antonio, Texas, a woman Baba befriended during his travels to the States after my mother's death.

Rashida wanders in now and then to bring me a cup of tea or merely to stare, as if to convince herself that Baba has not come back, as though he'd gone on a business trip to Delhi and might reappear at any moment. 'I knew he was going to die,' she says, not to me especially. 'I thought I was ready, but now that he is gone I still can't believe it.' The end of her shawl is wet from dabbing at her eyes.

The spare bed is covered with paint brushes, palette knives, tubes of paint, sketch pads, boxes of charcoal and pastels. The walls are lined with ranks of unfinished paintings. The fragrance of turpentine and linseed oil, a smell which in my childhood always meant Baba, hangs over everything.

I lie down exhausted on Baba's bed. I stare up at the blades of the ceiling fan. Despite the heat I do not dare to turn it on for fear of disordering the carefully sorted personal memorabilia and papers of no consequence to a dead man. Holy Jesus, I think, Rashida comes in to sit next to me on the bed. She fans me gently with a paper fan. 'Before I went to the States,' I tell her, 'I had an emptiness, a certain loneliness that I thought would pass with time.' I shift my weight and slip into the mould that Baba left in the polyfoam mattress. 'I thought it would be easy to leave it all behind.'

Rashida stares at me. 'You can never leave it all behind,' she says. 'A son is like a tree: the more branches it sprouts, the deeper grow the roots.'

I smile at her. 'And a daughter?'

She smiles back, a smile full of deliberate mystery and mischief, the smile of the child sister I left when I went to America. 'A daughter is like a river. Miles and miles it flows to merge with the sea, yet its banks remain unchanged.'

On Thursday, *Mamon* (Uncle) Majid, my mother's brother, dies unexpectedly of heart failure. It is as though the gods have repented making me miss my father's funeral and have kindly provided another in its place. After *Zuhr* (afternoon prayer) at the graveside, I see *Mamon* Majid's face for the last time. He lies in the coffin he brought back from his pilgrimage to Mecca, wound in a black sheet, only his face exposed. His head is bent slightly to the right, as though he died in the act of an ironic shrug. I bend over him and the pungent odour of camphor stings the back of my throat. He is pale, motionless, so very still, the way Baba must have looked. A big drop of perspiration slides off my nose, onto *Mamon* Majid's eyelid and rolls down his cheek. He looks as though he is crying.

The morning after *Mamon* Majid's funeral, Friday, the one-week anniversary of Baba's death, the sky remains dark with gusting winds blowing at near-hurricane force. Trees and utility poles are bent and uprooted, TV antennas blow like tumbleweed and billboards fly like pages of yesterday's newspaper. Half of Karachi loses electricity. Hail falls, giant frozen teardrops on the yellow grass. At last the rain comes in a great drowning torrent and the streets turn to rivers. Three members of a cricket team are electrocuted when their bus is stranded under a bridge and they walk on live power lines buried in the flood water.

As the lightning and thunder crash and the winds howl around the house, I pack for the return trip. Into my carry-on bag I put Baba's portrait of my mother and an unfinished self-portrait. I also take two of his books, a biography of Muhammad and the poetry of Ghalib, his silver betel tin, the letters of the renowned British artist and Baba's diary from 1930 to 1937. It is a thick black leather-bound notebook, with his name engraved in fading gold capital letters.

That evening, the weather calm once more, I leave on a non-stop flight to Amsterdam. At the gate, Rashida takes me in her arms and holds me for a long time. I feel her strength flowing into me, as though she is trying to transfuse me with it for the ordeal of my journey home. She tells me in a fierce whisper that she is afraid she will never see me again. I tease her, reassure her, make Asif promise to bring her when he visits me in New York next year. I think of what Baba used to say upon my frequent departures, 'Why leave if you are planning to come back?'

A bright sun shines over the clouds all the way from Amsterdam to New York. Virginia meets me at the airport, leaving Sean and Sarina with my cousin Azra, the one who gave me the mousetrap. Virginia kisses me gently, holds me close. 'I missed you,' she whispers. 'I'm glad you're home.' On the drive from Queens to Brooklyn, I watch a sunset dramatic enough for Hollywood: red sky, banks of purple clouds, radical oranges and violets dimming and drowning in the blackness which creeps from the east. On the car radio, Springsteen sings 'My Father's House.'

During the night, lying next to Virginia in the darkness that comes with sleep, everything becomes more real than waking life. It is sunrise and I am at the house on the banks of the River Jumna. Every door in the house is open, Asif's tricycle stands in the courtyard, the tea kettle on the stove has just stopped boiling. I walk from room to room. The beds are made up, covered with red, yellow and green quilts; Rashida's dolls sit on her bedroom shelf. I can sense them all there, the members of my family. As though they have just left each room as I enter it. I smell my mother's fragrance, the smoke of Baba's Passing Show cigarettes. I call out, but no one answers. I rush back into the courtyard and cross over to Baba's studio. The door stands wide and I find myself on the threshold of my own Brooklyn dining room. On the far side, across the gleaming expanse of dark oak floor, stands Baba, his back to me, working on a canvas. I feel a rush of indescribable joy. 'Baba!' I shout, and start across the room to embrace him. He turns to me, and there is a smile on his face of such ineffable love and sadness that I freeze in midstep. I call out again, but my feet are stuck, immobile on that fatal shiny expanse that stands between me and my father. It is only then that I see what he is painting: a self-portrait in a hall of mirrors, and the faces looking back at me from the canvas are Baba's, my own, and my son's.

Leaving the stranger who is my wife alone in bed, I sit in the living room of the unfamiliar house where my American children are growing up in a city as alien to me as the deserts of the moon. I drink coffee and chain-smoke, something I haven't done in years. I watch dawn come up over Brooklyn. One day soon, I tell myself, I shall write to the renowned artist in Lancaster, England, to Faye Dincin in San Antonio, Texas, and tell them that Baba is dead.

My Simple Little Brother and the Great Aversion Therapy Experiment
Lilith Norman

Little brother Fields drives the whole family mad by taking everything literally. However, a visit from Uncle Percy will sort him out – or will it?

> YEAR 7 TEACHING OBJECTIVES
> **R12 Comment, using appropriate terminology on how writers convey setting, character and mood through word choice and sentence structure.**
> **Wr19 Write reflectively about a text, taking account of the needs of others who might read it.**

1. Read the start of the story, as far as 'He'll grow out of it.' (page 2) How does the author establish the character of the narrator and the family in this section? For example, the repetition of the word 'DUMB' (page 1) gives the impression that the narrator is young and fed-up with his brother.

Pick out other quotations from the start of the story and explain how they help to establish the character of the narrator and the family.

2. A TV producer is looking for short stories to turn into one-off television programmes. You have been asked to read this story and write a report on whether or not it is suitable.

- In pairs, make a list of the things you think the producer would want to know about the story. Include all the features of good review writing that are relevant (clear paragraphing, clearly expressed and supported opinions, etc.).
- Using your list, write an individual review of the story, giving your opinions and explaining why it is or is not suitable.
- Exchange reviews with your partner. Read his/her piece and check whether they have covered all the points in your list.

Rules of the Game
Amy Tan

Vincent, is given a chess set for Christmas but it is his sister, Waverly Jong, who becomes the champion. She can see through the moves of her opponents – but cannot always cope with the complexities of family life.

YEAR 7 TEACHING OBJECTIVES
W8 Recognise and record personal errors, corrections, investigations, conventions, expectations and new vocabulary.
R12 Comment, using appropriate terminology on how writers convey setting, character and mood through word choice and sentence structure.
R17 Read a range of recent fiction texts independently as the basis for developing critical reflection and personal response.

---

1. From the story, identify words that you are likely to want to use in your own writing but that are not easy to spell. Write a list of these words in your spelling journal along with strategies to help you remember how to spell each one.

2. Skim read the story, looking for adjectives that you think are important in creating this story's mood. For each adjective, write a brief explanation of the connections and ideas which this word has for you and how these link with what the story is about.

3. Write about your response to this story. Include:
- reflections on what you like about the story
- how you feel about the ending
- your feelings about the characters
- questions you have about the story
- comparisons between this story and other things you have read.

Read another pupil's work and write a response to it, giving your thoughts on any questions they have about the story.

The Wardrobe, the Old Man and Death
Julio Ramón Ribeyro

The wardrobe is intriguing to the boys and a source of inspiration and comfort to their father. After an accident, this link with the past is broken and the past no longer haunts the family.

YEAR 7 TEACHING OBJECTIVES
R12 Comment, using appropriate terminology on how writers convey setting, character and mood through word choice and sentence structure.
S&L1 Use talk as a tool for clarifying ideas.

---

1. Select six words from paragraph 2 (pages 31–32) that you feel are important in establishing the mood of this story. Explain the links between these words and the mood of the story by developing six spider diagrams, one for each word, and show the connotations each word has for you.

2. Re-read the description of the football game, from 'Alberto junior sent his car underneath the bed ...' to '... and vanished into the depths of the house.' (pages 35–37). How does the author use word classes (adjectives, verbs, etc.) and sentence types (simple, complex, etc.) to establish the mood and setting here? Why do you think this mood is established?

3. In pairs, discuss what aspects of this story tell you it is from a different culture. What aspects of the story indicate that it is from a culture that has many features in common with British culture? Make notes on both issues as you talk. Share your ideas with another pair.

Big Bill
Satyajit Ray

Tulsi Babu cannot see what is special about a double rainbow. However, after finding a giant egg while walking through a forest, he is soon introduced to the wonders and terrors of nature.

YEAR 8 TEACHING OBJECTIVES
W4 Learn complex polysyllabic words and unfamiliar words which do not conform to regular patterns.
R10 Analyse the overall structure of a text to identify how key ideas are developed.
Wr5 Develop the use of commentary and description in narrative.

---

1. (a) In pairs, make a list of complex, polysyllabic words from this story. Divide them into syllables as in the following examples:
   colleague: coll/ea/gue
   sceptical: scep/ti/cal
   medicinal: med/i/cin/al
   (b) Now use 'look, say, cover, write, check' to learn these spellings. Develop a mnemonic for any words that give you particular problems.

2. Re-read the opening of the story, as far as '… part-time herbalist.' (page 42) and the last paragraph of the story (page 60).
   - How do the references to herbal medicine connect the beginning and the ending of this story?
   - How is Tulsi Babu's character described at the start of the story and how is his character important in the ending?

3. Re-write the ending of the story from 'Tulsi Babu's call resounded in the forest. "Bill! Bill! Billie!"' (page 58)
   Compare your new ending with one written by another pupil. Discuss how the two endings compare with the original.
   - How is the story's tension developed?
   - How do these new endings link up with details in the rest of the story?
   - Is the behaviour of the characters consistent with their behaviour in the rest of the story?

The Liar
Mulk Raj Anand

Labhu has a reputation as an excellent storyteller, hunter and liar. When he returns from a trip to the Himalayas the story he tells to explain his injured foot makes use of all these skills.

> YEAR 8 TEACHING OBJECTIVES
> **R13 Read a substantial text revising and refining interpretations of subject matter, style and technique.**
> **Wr5 Develop the use of commentary and description in narrative.**

1. (a) Read the first two paragraphs of the story (pages 61–62). Complete the following sentences:
- My first impressions of Labhu were ... because ... The author describes him as ... and this suggests to me that ...

(b) Now read the paragraph beginning 'When Labhu came back ...' (page 65) Complete the following sentence:
- On his return from the Himalayas, Labhu is described as ... which makes the reader think ...

(c) Read from 'On the eighth day ...' (page 67) to the end of the story. Complete the following sentences:
- At the end of the story Labhu ... This contrasts with ... The author uses ... to give the reader the feeling that ...

2. With a partner, make a list of questions that you would like to ask the author of this story. Make sure you cover the following aspects:
- the subject matter of the story
- the author's style and use of technique.

Now hot-seat the author. Are you convinced by the answers given?

3. Imagine you are Kuldeep Singh. Write your version of the hunting expedition with Labhu. You will need to consider the following questions:
- Were you as bad a hunter as Labhu suggests?
- How much game was shot and by whom?
- Did you or anyone else on the expedition see a wild monster or a princess of the royal house of Nepal?
- How did Labhu hurt his foot?

To Build a Fire
Jack London

A man and his dog set off through the intense cold of the Yukon. As the situation becomes increasingly desperate, advice from an older, more experienced man runs through the traveller's head, and the dog's instincts tell it that this is no time to be out.

YEAR 9 TEACHING OBJECTIVES
R7 Compare the presentation of ideas, values or emotions in related or contrasting texts.

1. Re-read the ending of the story from 'A certain fear of death, ...' (page 89) How does the author describe the man's death? Use the following headings to organise your ideas:
   - Description of his thoughts
   - Variation of sentence length
   - Description of his experience of the cold weather
   - The shift of narrative focus from the man to the dog

2. Compare this description of death with that of the young student in the story *Marriage of the Dead*. Are any of the same techniques used?

3. Early in the story the author writes 'The trouble with him was that he was without imagination.' (page 70) Work through the story, listing the pieces of advice given by 'That man from Sulphur Creek' (page 77) and the instinctive feelings of the dog. Against each, note down how the traveller actually behaves.

4. Compare how the theme of a lack of imagination is handled in this story and in *The Liar* and *Big Bill*.

Marriage of the Dead
Li Rui

In rural China, an old woman watches as a group of men dig up the bones of a dead girl. Superstitions are discussed as they work to honour the memory of this young, city woman who tried to help them.

YEAR 9 TEACHING OBJECTIVES

Sn7 Analyse and exploit the stylistic conventions of the main text types.

Wr5 Explore different ways of opening, structuring and ending narratives and experiment with narrative perspective.

---

1. How is the sentence structure of the inscription on the gravestone (pages 97–98) different from that of the rest of the story?

2. Re-read the first paragraph and the last two paragraphs of the story. What links are there between these sections? How would the story have been different if these sections had not been included?

3. Divide this story into five or six sections. On separate cards write a brief explanation of each section. Re-order the cards and consider the impact that the new order would have on the story. Discuss why the author chosen not to begin the story with the section that is set in the past?

4. The young woman in the story is sent out into rural China to help with agricultural developments as part of the Cultural Revolution. The story points out the hardship and suffering that was involved. What clues are there in the story that indicate that the author feels that the Cultural Revolution was a waste of time?

A Gentleman's Agreement
Elizabeth Jolley

A mother has two children – but they are good at nothing. The grandfather's land in the country makes no money but it cannot be sold until he dies. There seems to be no way out of the family's poverty.

YEAR 8 TEACHING OBJECTIVES
R3 Make notes in different ways, choosing a form which suits the purpose.
R4 Review their developing skills as active, critical readers who search for meaning using a range of reading strategies.

---

1. Work in pairs. Assess the woman's situation at the start and end of this story using SWOT analysis. List and analyse:
- the strengths and positive aspects of her position
- the weaknesses or negative aspects
- the opportunities available
- any threats.

Use a table like the one below to organise your ideas.

Strengths	Weaknesses
Opportunities	Threats

2. Analyse the structure of this story, concentrating on the timing of the different sections. Devise a flow diagram to represent the way the story is organised.

3. Write about the process of coming to an understanding of this story. You should try to cover the following points:
- Which activities have you done with the story and how have they helped you to understand it more completely?
- What reading techniques have you used to make sense of the story?
- What methods have helped you to understand the characters and their behaviour?
- What was the most useful way of sharing ideas about this story?

211

Private Eloy
Samuel Feijoo

Private Eloy joins the Cuban army to escape a life of poverty. However, his new role soon brings him into situations where desperate choices have to be made.

YEAR 8 TEACHING OBJECTIVES
R5 Trace the development of themes, values or ideas in texts.
R16 Recognise how texts refer to and reflect the culture in which they were produced.

---

1. As you read, write a series of journal entries in which you explain your reactions to the ideas and themes contained in the story. You should comment on:
- the title of the story and what this suggests to you
- Eloy's family and home situation
- the way Eloy gets into the army
- Eloy's reluctance to study and the impact of this decision
- the impact of the first eviction on Eloy
- the pressures on Eloy to stay in the army
- the advance
- Eloy's discovery of the wounded peasant and his decision to return to him.

2. Construct a timeline showing the main events in the story. Link quotations to the main events in the timeline and colour code them to pick out the key themes of the story.

3. What does this story tell you about life in Cuba? Collect information from the text under the following headings:
- Family life
- Wealth and poverty
- The landscape
- Race
- Government
- Education
- Employment

Once Upon a Time
Nadine Gordimer

The family live a perfect, fairy-tale life until their fears about the outside world begin to destroy the values they are trying to preserve.

YEAR 9 TEACHING OBJECTIVES

R7 Compare the presentation of ideas, values or emotions in related or contrasting texts.

Wr5 Explore different ways of opening, structuring and ending narratives and experiment with narrative perspective.

1. Read the first paragraph of this story again very carefully.
- What features of fairy stories can you find in the style and content of this opening?
- What other features are there here which suggest that this story is not going to conclude with a fairy story's traditional happy ending?

2. This story clearly presents the family and the decisions that they make in a negative way. Some of these negative features are listed in the table below. Look at the table. Discuss the entries and add further entries of your own.

Feature	How this is shown in a negative way (reader's view)	How this could be seen in a positive way (family's view)
They have electronically-controlled gates fitted.	It cuts them off from their own community.	It is a sensible security measure in the circumstances.
They do not employ any of the people who come asking for jobs.	It shows a lack of trust.	Only those with reliable references should be allowed to work in your house.

See Me in Me Benz and T'ing
Hazel D. Campbell

A rich Jamaican woman gets an urgent call from her husband. She has to drive to his factory. But this means driving through the poor parts of town.

YEAR 9 TEACHING OBJECTIVES
R6 Comment on the authorial perspectives offered in texts on individuals, community and society in texts from different cultures.
R7 Compare the presentation of ideas, values or emotions in related or contrasting texts.

---

1. In this story, the Lady of the house dislikes and is scared of the poor people who live in the area she has to drive through. These people are themselves angry with the Lady and others like her. What evidence is presented in the story to justify why these people feel as they do about each other?

2. What conclusions have you come to about the society described in this story? What do you think the author's intention was in writing this story?

3. This story and *Coffee for the Road* describe car journeys that go badly wrong. Using a table like the one below, compare these two stories, completing it with your own ideas.

	See Me in Me Benz and T'ing	*Coffee for the Road*
Ideas	•	•
Values	•	•
Emotions	The crowd lose their temper because of economic injustice.	The mother loses her temper after being treated in a racist manner.

Five Hours to Simla
Anita Desai

During a long car journey through the heat of northern India, a family are held up by a minor accident. The story examines the different responses and emotions that this delay evokes.

1. Focus on the opening of the story, up to '... a long, piercing wail emerged.' (page 147) How does the author use the five senses to evoke a very strong sense of a particular place in this opening passage? Discuss this question in pairs and put together a mind map to organise your responses.

2. This story is very clearly set in India. In pairs, skim read the story again, looking for details that place the story clearly in India. Record your findings in a table like the one below.

Feature of the story	Evidence that tells us this is India	What this tells us about Indian culture
Traffic		
Roads		
Landscape		
The family		
Cause of delay		
Response of travellers		
Response of locals		
Solution to problem		
Attitude to authority		

Coffee for the Road
Alex la Guma

As she drives south through the night from Johannesburg to Cape Town in apartheid South Africa, a mother becomes more and more tired. Her children ask for coffee, not knowing the trouble their demand would cause in this racially divided country.

YEAR 8 TEACHING OBJECTIVES

R10 Analyse the overall structure of a text to identify how key ideas are developed.

Wr6 Experiment with figurative language in conveying a sense of character and setting.

---

1. Make a list of images in the story that are used to describe the mother. Record them and the impression each one gives you about the woman in a table similar to the one below.

Image	Impression
'her eyes red, with the feeling of sand under the lids, irritating the eyeballs' (page 162)	She is tired and cross.

2. Identify the different settings used in the story and the points at which the focus shifts from one setting to another. How are the settings described and how do they add richness to the story? You may want to think about:
- imagery
- repetition
- use of long and short sentences
- vocabulary choices
- links between the settings and the different dialogues in the story.

3. This story contains many references to colour, both of people and things. Trace these references through the story and evaluate the impact of this device on the story's themes.

The Day Mr Prescott Died
Sylvia Plath

An elderly woman takes her daughter to the house of a friend whose husband has died earlier that day. The tense situation leads to some unexpected humour as we see the gathered mourners through the daughter's eyes.

YEAR 9 TEACHING OBJECTIVES

R6 Comment on the authorial perspectives offered in texts on individuals, community and society in texts from different cultures.

R12 Analyse and discuss the use made of rhetorical devices in a text.

---

1. The story is a first-person narrative from the point of view of the daughter. Make notes on the following topics in preparation for a discussion about how you feel about the narrator and how you think her mother feels about her. Support your ideas with reference to the text.
   - funerals
   - the neighbourhood
   - the relatives of the dead man and their behaviour
   - the daughter's sense of humour and how she speaks to people.

2. What view does this story present of the society in which it takes place? Is it described in a warm way or is the tone resentful? Consider:
   - the physical description of the locality
   - the general description of the people
   - the relationships between the people and their support for one another
   - the society's attitudes, traditions and values
   - the people's approach to death.

3. Consider the dialogue of the story. How has the author given her characters words that:
   - show us they are from America
   - indicate how they feel about each other?
   To answer these questions you will need to think carefully about individual words and the effects created by the way the words are put together.

From Brooklyn to Karachi via Amsterdam
S. Afzal Haider

When the narrator journeys back to his homeland to see his dying father, he is taken back to his roots and made to re-assess his life.

YEAR 9 TEACHING OBJECTIVES

R16 Analyse ways in which different cultural contexts and traditions have influenced language and style.

Wr3 Produce formal essays in standard English within a specified time, writing fluently and legibly and maintaining technical accuracy when writing at speed.

---

1. New York and Karachi are the two main settings for this story. The differences between these two cities is one of the central themes of the story. Re-read the story collecting details of life in these two places. You should include:
   - religion
   - weather
   - attitudes to death
   - family life
   - the physical experience of living in each place.

   How does what the narrator says about one city influence your view of the other?

2. There are many quotations from the Koran and references to Pakistani names, phrases and sayings in this story.
   (a) Make a list of linguistic references to Pakistani life.
   (b) Take three examples from your list and write a detailed explanation of why the author has included them in the story and what impact they have on you as a reader.

3. How and to what effect does *From Brooklyn to Karachi via Amsterdam* portray the cultures of Asia and North America? Write a formal essay on this topic, taking no longer than one hour (including planning and checking time). Use the work you have done for Activities 1 and 2 as preparation.

Further reading

Other books by authors in this collection

Climb a Lonely Hill by Lilith Norman
(Random House Australia, 1996) (ISBN: 0091830206)
A story about a boy and a girl who are stranded in the Australian desert after a car accident.

The Joy Luck Club by Amy Tan
(Vintage, 1989) (ISBN: 0749399570)
The story of four Chinese mothers who form the mah-jong playing social and investment club in San Francisco, interlaced with the stories of their Americanised daughters.

The Call of the Wild by Jack London
(Puffin Books, 1994) (ISBN: 0140366695)
Buck is sold to be a sledge dog in the frozen north wastes of North America. But Buck escapes to lead a wolf pack and becomes a legend of the north.

Stories by Elizabeth Jolley
(Penguin Books, 1989) (ISBN: 0140085815)
A collection of stories by Elizabeth Jolley, including an autobiographical piece describing the people and things that have influenced the author.

Jump and Other Stories by Nadime Gordimer
(Bloomsbury, 1991) (ISBN: 0747511896)
A collection of stories that takes the reader on a journey across cultures, from Mozambique to the south of France.

Singerman by Hazel D. Campbell
(Peepal Tree Press, 1991) (ISBN: 0948833440)
A collection of short stories about Caribbean people, focussing on the issues of race, class and poverty.

The Village by the Sea by Anita Desai
(Puffin Books, 2001) (ISBN: 0141312718)
With their mother ill and their father permanently drunk, Hara and Lila have to earn money to keep the house and look after their two young sisters.

Johnny Panic and the Bible of Dreams, and Other Prose Writings by Sylvia Plath
(Faber and Faber, 1977) (ISBN: 0571049893)
A wonderful collection of short stories which will keep you guessing what will happen in each story.

Books with similar themes by other authors

Journey to the River Sea by Eva Ibbotson
(Longman, 2003) (ISBN: 0582795923)
The story of Maia's extraordinary adventures in the Amazon rainforest.

Chinese Cinderella by Adeline Yen Mah
(Longman, 2002) (ISBN: 0582447224)
Adeline Yen Mah's vivid autobiography describes her life growing up in China at the time of the Cultural Revolution.

Journey to Jo'burg by Beverley Naidoo
(Longman, 2000) (ISBN: 0582434513)
Thirteen-year-old Naledi's mother lives and works in Johannesburg, 300 kilometres away from her home village and children. When Dineo, Naledi's baby sister falls ill, Naledi knows she must find her mother so she and her brother set out on foot on their eye-opening journey.

Glossary

My Simple Little Brother
2   **coddle:** pamper
     galvanized: metal coated in zinc to stop it rusting
     heifers: young cows
3   **sulky:** a two-wheeled carriage for one person
4   **luscious:** delicious
5   **aversion:** dislike
6   **conchology:** the study of molluscs and their shells
8   **ultrasonic:** high-frequency sound, inaudible to humans

Rules of the Game
15   **Caucasian:** a white person
21   **benevolently:** generously
     retort: quick or funny response
22   **etiquette:** rules and manners
24   **Tao:** a Chinese religion
25   **barrettes:** hair clips in the shape of a bar
     malodorous: bad smelling
27   **careened:** rolled on their sides

The Wardrobe, the Old Man and Death
31   **baroque:** a bold, ornamental style of architecture
     curlicues: extravagant curls or twists
     protean: able to change shape
     blackjack: a short club
36   **spectral:** ghostly

Big Bill
42   **hypertension:** high blood pressure
     allopathy: orthodox medical practice
43   **Sanskrit:** the ancient language of India

45	**bulbul:** a singing bird similar to a nightingale
46	**dhoti:** a loin cloth
48	**malevolent:** ill-wishing
49	**rudimentary:** simple, elementary
54	**shikaris:** hunters
60	**masticate:** chew

The Liar

61	**Shikari:** hunter
63	*oorial*: a wild sheep of the Himalayas
	chimaera: a legendary monster made up of sections from different animals
	vouchsafed: graciously given
64	**chagrined:** annoyed
	malicious: spiteful, full of bad thoughts
65	**garrulous:** talkative
66	**purblind:** almost blind

To Build a Fire

69	**pall:** covering
	undulations: small wave-like shapes
70	*chechaquo*: a tenderfoot, someone who is inexperienced
	conjectural: involving guess-work or unproven ideas
75	**candied:** encrusted with sugar
88	**peremptorily:** not allowing discussion or disagreement

Marriage of the Dead

93	**hoary:** grey or white with age
	temporised: tried to gain time
94	**tallied:** agreed, were compatible
101	**cowed:** subdued, depressed
	dotard: fool
103	**bole:** trunk of a tree

A Gentleman's Agreement

106 **feckless:** helpless

108 **furze:** gorse

112 **carter:** cart driver

113 **jarrah:** tree from Western Australia, grown for timber

Private Eloy

115 **mulatto:** a person with one black and one white parent

Galician: descended from people of Galicia in Spain

116 *guajiro:* peasant

117 *guayabera:* loose shirt

pesos: coins of little value

118 **lianas:** climbing plants

121 **despotism:** tyrannical rule

124 **vanguard:** soldiers nearest the front

Once Upon a Time

127 **itinerant:** travelling

129 **keening:** wailing over the body of a dead person

cicadas: insects that make loud chirping sounds

harpies: a mythical monster; half woman, half bird

audaciously: daringly

importuned: repeatedly asked for

baas: master

130 *tsotsis:* a young black South African thug

131 **aesthetics:** the principles of art and good taste

neo-classical: a revival of Roman and Greek style of architecture

facades: the front, outside part of a building

132 **serrations:** saw-like teeth shapes

cornice: a ridge or projection along the top of a building

See Me in Me Benz and T'ing

139   **fassing:** meddling
        gyrating: spinning around, dancing
140   **cotching:** catching up
142   **ducoman:** handyman

Five Hours to Simla

145   **Rexine:** imitation leather cloth
148   **kohl:** a fine black powder used as eye make-up
149   **paisa:** an Indian coin of small value
151   **culvert:** arched water channel beneath a road
153   **jounced:** jolted, shook
154   *thana*: police station

Coffee for the Road

162   **fatigued:** tired
        strata: layers
164   *koppies*: low hills
        dongas: gullies
165   **corrals:** animal enclosures
166   **nondescript:** unexceptional

The Day Mr Prescott Died

175   **jouncing:** jolting, shaking
179   **portières:** curtains hung over a doorway

From Brooklyn to Karachi via Amsterdam

188   **tumour:** swelling or growth
        lobotomy: an operation, usually on the brain
194   *Sahib*: a respectful form of address, similar to Sir
        enervated: sapped of all strength
197   **muezzin:** person who calls other Muslims to prayer
201   **pungent:** sharp-smelling
        camphor: solid aromatic oil from laurel trees
        betel: a leaf for chewing

Acknowledgements

We are grateful to the following for permission to reproduce copyright material:

Faber & Faber for the story "The Day Mr Prescott Died" by Sylvia Plath published in *Johnny Panic and the Bible of Dreams*; Syed Afzal Haider for the story "From Brooklyn to Karachi via Amsterdam" by Syed Afzal Haider published in *Sacred Ground* by Milkweed Press © Syed Afzal Haider; A.M Health & Co for the story "The Wardrobe, the Old Man and Death" by Julio Ramon Ribeyro translated by Nick Caistor © 1998 Macmillan Publishers Ltd, from *The Picador Book of Latin American Stories* ed Carols Fuentes and Julio Ortega; Margaret Connolly & Associates Pty Ltd for the story "My Simple Little Brother" by Lilith Norman published in *My Simple Little Brother*; Viking Penguin Group USA Inc for the Story "A Gentleman's Agreement" by Elizabeth Jolley published in *Stories* © 1976, 1979, 1984 Elizabeth Jolley; Orient Paperbacks for the stories "Five hours to Simla" by Anita Desai published in *Diamond Dust and Other Stories* and "The Lair" by Mulk Raj Anand published in *A Pair of Mustachios and Other Stories* © Mulk Raj Anand; Sandra Dijkstra Literacy Agency for the extract "Rules of the Game" by Amy Tan published in *The Joy Luck Club* © Amy Tan 1992; Savacou Publications for the story "See me in me Benz and T'ing" by Hazel D Campbell published in *West Indian Stories*; A.P Watt Ltd and Penguin Group (Canada) for the story "Once Upon a Time" by